THE MAN
IN THE
PICTURE

Other books by Susan Hill

NOVELS

The Woman in Black
In the Sprngtime of the Year
I'm the King of the Castle
The Bird of Night

SHORT STORIES

The Boy who Taught the Beekeper to read and other Stories

CRIME NOVELS

The Various Haunts of Men
The Pure in Heart
The Risk of Darkness

THE MAN IN THE PICTURE

SUSAN HILL

PROFILE BOOKS

This paperback edition published in 2008

First published in Great Britain in 2007 by
PROFILE BOOKS LTD
3A Exmouth House
Pine Street
London EC1R 0JH
www.profilebooks.com

5 7 9 10 8 6 4

Printed and bound in Great Britain by
Clays Ltd, St Ives plc

Designed in Fournier by Geoff Green Book Design, Cambridge

The moral right of the author has been asserted.

A CIP catalogue record for this book is available from the British Library.

ISBN 978 1 84668 544 6

FSC
www.fsc.org
MIX
Paper from
responsible sources
FSC® C018072

Stephen Mallatratt
Remembered with love and gratitude

THE MAN IN THE PICTURE

PROLOGUE

HE STORY was told to me by my old tutor, Theo Parmitter, as we sat beside the fire in his college rooms one bitterly cold January night. There were still real fires in those days, the coals brought up by the servant in huge brass scuttles. I had travelled down from London to see my old friend, who was by then well into his eighties, hale and hearty and with a mind as sharp as ever, but crippled by severe arthritis so that he had difficulty leaving his rooms. The college looked after him well. He was one of a dying breed, the old Cambridge bachelor for whom his college was his family. He had lived in this handsome set for over fifty years and he would be content to die here. Meanwhile a number of us, his old pupils from

several generations back, made a point of visiting him from time to time, to bring news and a breath of the outside world. For he loved that world. He no longer went out into it much but he loved the gossip – to hear who had got what job, who was succeeding, who was tipped for this or that high office, who was involved in some scandal.

I had done my best to entertain him most of the afternoon and through dinner, which was served to us in his rooms. I would stay the night, see a couple of other people and take a brisk walk round my old stamping grounds, before returning to London the following day.

But I should not like to give the impression that this was a sympathy visit to an old man from whom I gained little in return. On the contrary, Theo was tremendous company, witty, acerbic, shrewd, a fund of stories which were not merely the rambling reminiscences of an old man. He was a wonderful conversationalist – people, even the youngest Fellows, had always vied to sit next to him at dinner in hall.

Now, it was the last week of the vacation and the

college was quiet. We had eaten a good dinner, drunk a bottle of good claret, and we were stretched out comfortably in our chairs before a good fire. But the winter wind, coming as always straight off the Fens, howled round and occasionally a burst of hail rattled against the glass.

Our talk had been winding down gently for the past hour. I had told all my news, we had set the world to rights between us, and now, with the fire blazing up, the edge of our conversation had blunted. It was delightfully cozy sitting in the pools of light from a couple of lamps and for a few moments I had fancied that Theo was dozing.

But then he said, 'I wonder if you would care to hear a strange story?'

'Very much.'

'Strange and somewhat disturbing.' He shifted in his chair. He never complained of it but I suspected that the arthritis gave him considerable pain. 'The right sort of tale for such a night.'

I glanced across at him. His face, caught in the flicker of the firelight, had an expression so serious – I would almost say deathly serious – that I was startled. 'Make of it what you will, Oliver,' he said quietly, 'but I assure you of this, the story is true.'

He leaned forward. 'Before I begin, could I trouble you to fetch the whisky decanter nearer?'

I got up and went to the shelf of drinks, and as I did so, Theo said, 'My story concerns the picture to your left. Do you remember it at all?'

He was indicating a narrow strip of wall between two bookcases. It was in heavy shadow. Theo had always been known as something of a shrewd art collector with some quite valuable old-master drawings and eighteenth-century water-colours, all picked, he had once told me, for modest sums when he was a young man. I do not know much about paintings, and his taste was not really mine. But I went over to the picture he was pointing out.

'Switch on the lamp there.'

Although it was a somewhat dark oil painting, I now saw it quite well and looked at it with interest. It was of a Venetian carnival scene. On a landing stage beside the Grand Canal and in the square behind it, a crowd in masks and cloaks milled around among entertainers – jugglers and tumblers and musicians and more people were climbing into gondolas, others already out on the water, the boats bunched together, with the gondoliers clashing poles. The picture was typical of those whose scenes are lit by flares and torches which throw an uncanny glow here and there, illuminating faces and patches of bright clothing and the silver ripples on the water, leaving other parts in deep shadow. I thought it had an artificial air but it was certainly an accomplished work, at least to my inexpert eye.

I switched off the lamp and the picture, with its slightly sinister revellers, retreated into its corner of darkness again.

'I don't think I ever took any notice of it before,' I said now, pouring myself a whisky. 'Have you had it long?'

'Longer than I have had the right to it.'

Theo leaned back into his deep chair so that he too was now in shadow. 'It will be a relief to tell someone. I have never done so and it has been a burden. Perhaps you would not mind taking a share of the load?'

I had never heard him speak in this way, never known him sound so deathly serious, but of course I did not hesitate to say that I would do anything he wished, never imagining what taking, as he called it, 'a share of the load' would cost me.

ONE

MY STORY really begins some seventy years ago, in my boyhood. I was an only child and my mother died when I was three. I have no memory of her. Nowadays, of course, my father might well have made a decent fist of bringing me up himself, at least until he met a second wife, but times were very different then, and although he cared greatly for me, he had no idea how to look after a boy scarcely out of nappies, and so a series of nurses and then nannies were employed. I have no tale of woe, of cruelty and harm at their hands. They were all kindly and well-meaning enough, all efficient, and though I remember little of them, I feel a general warmth towards them and the way they steered me into young boyhood. But my mother had had a sister, married to a wealthy man with considerable land and properties in Devon, and from the age of seven or so I spent many holidays with them and idyllic times they were. I was allowed to roam free, I enjoyed the company of local boys – my aunt and uncle had no children but my uncle had an adult son from his first marriage, his wife having died giving birth – and of the surrounding tenant farmers, the villagers, the ploughmen and black-smiths, grooms and hedgers and ditchers. I grew up healthy and robust as a result of spending so much time outdoors. But when I was not about the coun-tryside, I was enjoying a very different sort of edu-cation indoors. My aunt and uncle were cultured people, surprisingly widely and well read and with a splendid library. I was allowed the run of this as much as I was allowed the run of the estate and I followed their example and became a voracious reader. But my aunt was also a great connoisseur of pictures. She loved English watercolours but also had a broad, albeit traditional, taste for the old masters, and though she could not afford to buy paintings by the great names, she had acquired a good collection of minor artists. Her husband took little interest in this area, but he was more than happy to fund her passion, and seeing that I showed an early liking for certain pictures about the place, Aunt Mary jumped at the chance of bringing someone else up to share her enthusiasm. She began to talk to me about the pictures and to encourage me to read about the artists, and I very quickly understood the delight she took in them and had my own particular favourites among them. I loved some of the great seascapes and also the watercolours of the East Anglia school, the wonderful skies and flat fens – I think my taste in art had a good deal to do with my pleasure in the outside world. I could not warm to portraits or still lifes – but nor did Aunt Mary and there were few of them about. Interiors and pictures of churches left me cold and a young boy does not understand the charms of the human figure. But she encouraged me to be open to everything, not to copy her taste but to develop my own and always to wait to be surprised and challenged as well as delighted by what I saw.

I owe my subsequent love of pictures entirely to Aunt Mary and those happy, formative years. When she died, just as I was coming up to Cambridge, she left me many of the pictures you see around you now and others, too, some of which I sold in order to buy different ones — as I know she would have wished me to do. She was an unsentimental woman and she would have wanted me to keep my collection alive, to enjoy the business of acquiring new when I had tired of the old.

In short, for some twenty years or more I became quite a picture dealer, going to auctions regularly and in the process of having fun at the whole business building up more capital than I could ever have enjoyed on my academic salary. In between my forays into the art world, of course, I worked my way slowly up the academic ladder, establishing myself here in the college and publishing the books you know. I missed my regular visits to Devon once my aunt and uncle were dead, and I could only make sure I maintained my ties to a country way of life by regular walking holidays.

❧❧

I have sketched in my background and you now know a little more about my love of pictures. But what happened one day you could never guess and perhaps you will never believe the story. I can only repeat what I assured you of at the start. It is true.

TWO

<figure>ornament</figure>

IT WAS A BEAUTIFUL day at the beginning of the Easter vacation and I had gone up to London for a couple of weeks, to work in the Reading Room of the British Museum and to do some picture dealing. On this particular day there was an auction, with viewing in the morning, and from the catalogue I had picked out a couple of old-master drawings and one major painting which I particularly wanted to see. I guessed that the painting would go for a price far higher than I could afford but I was hopeful of the drawings and I felt buoyant as I walked from Bloomsbury down to St James's, in the spring sunshine. The magnolias were out, as were the cherry blossom, and set against the white stucco of the eighteenth-century terraces they were gay enough to lift the heart. Not that my heart was ever down. I was cheerful and optimistic when I was younger – indeed, in general I have been blessed with a sunny and equable temperament – and I enjoyed my walk and was keenly anticipating the viewing and the subsequent sale. There was no cloud in the sky, real or metaphorical.

The painting was not, in fact, as good as had been made out and I did not want to bid for it, but I was keen to buy at least one of the drawings, and I also saw a couple of watercolours which I knew I could sell on and I thought it likely that they would not fetch high prices because they were not the kind of pictures for which many of the dealers would be coming to this particular sale. I marked them off in the catalogue and went on wandering round.

Then, slightly hidden by a rather overpowering pair of religious panels, that Venetian oil of the carnival scene caught my eye. It was in poor condition, it badly needed cleaning and the frame was chipped in several places. It was not, indeed, the sort of picture I generally liked, but there was a strange, almost hallucinatory quality about it and I found myself looking at it for a long time and coming back to it, several times. It seemed to draw me into itself so that I felt a part of the night-time scene, lit by the torches and lanterns, one of the crowd of masked revellers, or of the party boarding a gondola and sailing over the moonlit canal and off into the darkness under an ancient bridge. I stood in front of it for a long time, peering into every nook and cranny of the palazzi with their shutters opening here and there on to rooms dark save for the light of a branch of candles here, a lamp there, the odd shadowy figure just glimpsed in the reflected light. The faces of the revellers were many of them the classic Venetian, with prominent noses, the same faces that could be seen as Magi and angels, saints and popes, in the great paintings that filled Venice's churches. Others, though, were recognizably of different nationalities and there was the occasional Ethiopian and Arab. I absorbed the picture in a way I had not done for a long time.

The sale began at two and I went out into the spring sunshine to find some refreshment before returning to the auction rooms, but as I sat in the dim bar of a quiet pub, through the windows of which the sun lanced here and there, I was still immersed in that Venetian scene. I knew of course that I had to buy the picture. I could barely enjoy my lunch and became agitated in case something happened to prevent my getting back to the rooms to bid, so I was one of the first there. But for some reason, I wanted to be standing at the back, away from the rostrum, and I hovered close to the door as the room began to fill. There were some important pictures and I caught sight of several well-known dealers who would be there on behalf of well-to-do clients. No one knew me.

The painting I had at first come to bid for was sold for more than I had expected, and the drawings went quickly beyond my means, but I was almost successful in obtaining a fine Cotman watercolour which came immediately after them when some of the buyers for the lots in the first half had left. I secured a small group of good seascapes and then sat through one stodgy sporting oil after another — fat men on horseback, huntsmen, horses with docked tails giving them an odd, unbalanced air, horses rearing, horses being held by bored grooms, on and on they went and up and up went the sea of hands. I almost dozed off. But then, as the sale was petering out, there was the Venetian carnival scene, looking dark and unattractive now that it was out in the open. There were a couple of half-hearted bids and then a pause. I raised my hand. No one took me on. The hammer was just coming down when there was a slight flurry behind me and a voice called out. I glanced round, surprised and dismayed that I should have last-minute competition for the Venetian picture, but the auctioneer took the view that the hammer had indeed fallen on my bid and there was an end to it. It was mine for a very modest sum.

The palms of my hands were damp and my heart was pounding. I have never felt such an anxiety — indeed, it was close to a desperation to obtain anything and I felt oddly shaken, with relief and also with some other emotion I could not identify. Why did I want the picture so badly? What was its hold over me?

As I went out of the saleroom towards the cashier's office to pay for my purchases, someone tapped me on the shoulder. I turned and saw a stout, sweating man carrying a large leather portfolio case.

'Mr ...?' he asked.

I hesitated.

'I need to speak with you urgently.'

'If you will forgive me, I want to get to the cashier's office ahead of the usual queue ...'

'No. Please do not.'

'I beg your pardon?'

'You must listen to what I have to say first. Is there somewhere we can go so as not to be overheard?' He was glancing around him as if he expected a dozen eavesdroppers to be closing in on us and I felt annoyed. I did not know the man and had no wish to scurry off with him to some corner.

'Anything you have to say to me can surely be said here. Everyone is busy about their own affairs. Why should they be interested in us?' I wanted to secure my purchases, arrange for them to be delivered to me, and be done.

'Mr ...' he paused again.

'Parmitter,' I said curtly.

'Thank you. My name is not relevant – I am acting on behalf of a client. I should have been here far earlier but I encountered a road accident, some unfortunate knocked over and badly injured by a speeding car and I was obliged to stay and speak to the police, it made me too late, I ...' He took out a large handkerchief and wiped his brow and upper lip but the beads of sweat popped up again at once. 'I have a commission. There is a picture ... I have to acquire it. It is absolutely vital that I take it back with me.'

'But you were too late. Bad luck. Still, it was hardly your fault — your client cannot reasonably blame you for witnessing a road accident.'

He looked increasingly uncomfortable and was sweating even more. I made to move away but he grabbed me and held me by the arm so fiercely that it was painful.

'The last picture,' he said, his breath foetid in my face, 'the Venetian scene. You obtained it and I must have it. I will pay you what you ask, with a good profit, you will not lose. It is in your interests after all, you would only sell it on later. What is your price?'

I wrenched my arm from his grip. 'There is none. The picture is not for sale.'

'Don't be absurd man, my client is wealthy, you can name your price. Don't you understand me — I *have to have that picture.*'

I had heard enough. Without troubling about good manners, I turned on my heel and walked away from him.

But he was there again, pawing at me, keeping close to my side. 'You have to sell the picture to me.'

'If you do not take your hands off I will be obliged to call the porters.'

'My client gave me instructions … I was not to go back without the picture. It has taken years to track it down. I have to have it.'

We had reached the cashier's office, where there was now, of course, a considerable queue of buyers waiting to pay. 'For the last time,' I hissed at him, 'let me alone. I have told you. I want the picture. I bought it and I intend to keep it.'

He took a step back and, for a moment, I thought that was that, but then he leaned close to me and said, 'You will regret it. I have to warn you. You will not want to keep that picture.'

His eyes bulged, and the sweat was running down his face now. 'Do you understand? Sell me the picture. It is for your own good.'

It was all I could do not to laugh in his face but, instead, I merely shook my head and turned away from him, to stare at the grey cloth of the jacket belonging to the man in front of me as if it were the most fascinating thing in the world.

I dared not look round again but by the time I had left the cashier's window having paid for my purchases, including the Venetian picture, the man was nowhere to be seen.

I was relieved and dismissed the incident from my

mind as I went out into the sunshine of St James's.

It was only later that evening, as I was settling down to work at my desk, that I felt a sudden, strange frisson, a chill down my spine. I had not been in the least troubled by the man — he had clearly been trying to make up some tale about the picture to convince me I should let him have it. Nevertheless, I felt uneasy.

Everything I had bought at the auction was delivered the next day and the first thing I did was take the Venetian picture across London to a firm of restorers. They would clean it expertly, and either repair the old frame or find another. I also took one of the others to have a small chip made good and because picture restorers work slowly, as they should, I did not see the paintings again for some weeks, by which time I had returned here to the Cambridge summer term that was in full swing.

I brought all the new pictures with me. I was in my London rooms too infrequently to leave anything of much value or interest there. I placed the rest with ease but wherever I put the Venetian picture it looked wrong. I have never had such trouble hanging a painting. And about one thing I was adamant. I did not want it in the room where I slept.

I did not even take it into the bedroom. Yet I am not a superstitious man, and up until that time had only ever suffered nightmares if I was ill and had a fever. Because I had such trouble finding the right place for it, in the end I left the painting propped up there, against the bookcase. And I could not stop looking at it. Every time I came back into these rooms, it drew me. I spent more time looking at it – no, into it – than I did with pictures of far greater beauty and merit. I seemed to need it, to spend far too much time looking into every corner, every single face.

I did not hear any more from the tiresome pest in the auction rooms, and I soon forgot about him entirely.

Just one curious thing happened around that time. It was in the autumn of the same year, the first week of Michaelmas term and a night when the first chills of autumn had me ring for a fire. It was blazing up well, and I was working at my desk, in the circle of lamplight, when I happened to glance up for a second. The Venetian painting was directly in my sight and something about it made me look more closely. Cleaning had revealed fresh depths to the picture, and much more detail was now clear. I could see far more people who were crowded on the path beside the water, several rows deep in places, and gondolas and other craft laden with revellers, some masked, others not, on the canal. I had studied the faces over and over again, and each time I found more. People hung out of windows and over balconies, more were in the dim recesses of rooms in the palazzi. But now, it was only one person, one figure, which caught my eye and stood out from all the rest, and although he was near the front of the picture, I did not think I had noticed the man before. He was not looking at the lagoon or the boats, but rather away from them and out of the scene – he seemed, in fact, to be looking at me, and into this room. He wore clothes of the day but plain ones, not the elaborate fancy dress of many of the carnival-goers, and he was not masked. But two of the revellers close to him wore masks and both appeared to have their hands upon him, one on his shoulder, the other round his left wrist, almost as if they were trying to keep a hold of him or even pull him back. His face had a strange expression, as if he were at once astonished and afraid. He was looking away from the scene because he did not want to be part of it and into my room, at me – at anyone in front of the picture – with what I can only describe as pleading. But for what? What was he asking? The shock was seeing a man's figure there at all when I had previously not noticed it. I supposed that the lamplight, cast on the painting at a particular angle, had revealed the figure clearly for the first time. Whatever the reason, his expression distressed me and I could not work with my former deep concentration. In the night, I woke several times, and, once, out of a strange dream in which the man in the picture was drowning in the canal and stretching out his arms for me to save him, and so vivid was the dream that I got out of bed and came in here, switched on the lamp and looked at the picture. Of course nothing had changed. The man was not drowning though he still looked at me, still pleaded, and I felt that he had been depicted trying to get away from the two men who had their hands on him.

I went back to bed.

And that, for a very long time, was that. Nothing more happened. The picture stayed propped up on the bookcase for months until eventually I found a space for it there, where you see it now.

I did not dream about it again. But it never lessened its hold on me, its presence was never anything but powerful, as if the ghosts of all those people in that weirdly lit, artificial scene were present with me, forever in the room.

Some years passed. The painting did not lose any of its strange force but of course everyday life goes on and I became used to it. I often spent time looking at it though, staring at the faces, the shadows, the buildings, the dark rippling waters of the Grand Canal, and I also vowed that one day I would go to Venice. I have never been a great traveller, as you know; I love the English countryside too much and never wanted to venture far from it during vacations. Besides, in those days I was busy teaching here, performing more and more duties within the college, researching and publishing a number of books and continuing to buy and sell some pictures, though my time for that was limited.

Only one odd thing happened concerning the picture during that period. An old friend, Brammer, came to visit me here. I had not seen him for some years and we had a great deal to talk about but at one point, soon after his arrival and while I was out of the room, he started to look round at the pictures. When I returned, he was standing in front of the Venetian scene and peering closely at it.

'Where did you come by this, Theo?'

'Oh, in a saleroom some years ago. Why?'

'It is quite extraordinary. If I hadn't ...' He shook his head. 'No.'

I went to stand beside him. 'What?'

'You know about all this sort of thing. When do you suppose it was painted?'

'It's late eighteenth century.'

He shook his head. 'Then I can't make it out. You see, that man there ...' He pointed to one of the figures in the nearest gondola. 'I ... I know – knew him. That's to say it is the absolute likeness of someone I knew well. We were young men together. Of course it cannot be him ... but everything – the way he holds his head, the expression ... it is quite uncanny.'

'With so many billions of people born and all of us only having two eyes, one nose, one mouth, I suppose it is even more remarkable that there are not more identical.'

But Brammer was not paying me any attention. He was too absorbed in studying the painting, and in scrutinizing that one face. It took me a while to draw him away from it and to divert him back to the topics of our earlier conversation, and several times over the next twenty-four hours he went back to the picture and would stand there, an expression of concern and disbelief on his face, shaking his head from time to time.

There was no further incident and, after a while, I put Brammer's strange discovery if not out of, then well to the back of my mind.

Perhaps, if I had not been the subject of an article in a magazine more general than academic, some years later, there would have been nothing else and so the story, such as it was until then, would have petered out.

I had completed a long work on Chaucer and it happened that there was a major anniversary which included an exhibition at the British Museum. There had also been an important manuscript discovery relating to his life, about which we have always known so little. The general press took an interest and there was a gratifying amount of attention given to my beloved poet. I was delighted of course.

I had long wanted to share the delights his work afforded with a wider public and my publisher was pleased when I agreed to be interviewed here and there.

One of the interviewers who came to see me brought a photographer and he took several pictures in these rooms. If you would care to go to the bureau and open the second drawer, you will find the magazine article filed there.

THREE

HEO WAS A meticulous man — everything was filed and ordered. I had always been impressed, coming in here to tutorials, and seeing the exemplary tidiness of his desk by comparison with that of most other fellows — not to mention with my own. It was a clue to the man. He had an ordered mind. In another life, he ought to have been a lawyer.

The cutting was exactly where he had indicated. It was a large spread about Theo, Chaucer, the exhibition and the new discovery, highly informed and informative, and the photograph of him, which took up a full page, was not only an excellent likeness of him as he had been some thirty years previously, but a fine composition in its own right. He was sitting in an armchair, with a pile of books on a small table beside him, his spectacles on top. The sun was slanting through the high window onto him and lighting the whole scene quite dramatically.

'This is a fine photograph, Theo.'

'Look though – look at where the sun falls.'

It fell onto the Venetian picture, which hung behind him, illuminating it vividly and in a strange harmony of light and dark. It seemed to be far more than a mere background.

'Extraordinary.'

'Yes. I confess I was quite taken aback when I saw it. I suppose by then I had grown used to the picture and I had no idea it had such presence in the room.'

I looked round. Now, the painting was half hidden, half in shade, and seemed a small thing, not attracting any attention. The figures were a little stiff and distant, the light rippling on the water dulled. It was like someone in a group who is so retiring and plain that he or she merges into the background unnoticed. What I saw in the magazine photograph was almost a different canvas, not in its content, which was of course the same, but in – I might almost say, in its attitude.

'Odd, is it not?' Theo was watching me intently.

'Did the photographer remark on the picture? Did he deliberately arrange it behind you and light it in some particular way?'

'No. It was never mentioned. He fussed a little with the table of books, I remember ... making the pile regular, then irregular ... and he had me shift about in the chair. That was all. I recall that when I saw the results – and there were quite a number of shots of course – I was very surprised. I had not even realized the painting was there. Indeed ...' He paused.

'Yes?'

He shook his head. 'It is something, to be frank, that has played on my mind ever since, especially in the light of ... subsequent events.'

'What is that?'

But he did not answer. I waited. His eyes were closed and he was quite motionless. I realized that the evening had exhausted him, and after waiting a little longer in the silence of those rooms, I got up and left, trying to make my exit soundless, and went away down the dark stone staircase and out into the court.

FOUR

I T WAS A STILL, clear and bitter night with a frost and a sky thick and brilliant with stars and I went quickly across to my own staircase to fetch my coat. It was late but I felt like fresh air and a brisk walk. The court was deserted and there were only one or two lights shining out from sets of rooms here and there.

The night porter was already installed in his lodge with a fire in the grate and a great brown pot of tea.

'You mind your step, sir, the pavements have a rime on them even now.'

I thanked him and went out through the great gate. King's Parade was deserted, the shops shuttered. A solitary policeman on the beat nodded to me as I passed him. I was intent on both keeping warm and staying upright as the porter had been right that the pavements were slippery here and there.

But quite without warning, I stopped because a sense of fear and oppression came over me like a wave of fever, so that a shudder ran through my body. I glanced round but the lane was empty and still. The fear I felt was not of anyone or anything, it was just an anonymous, unattached fear and I was in its grip. It was combined with a sense of impending doom, a dread, and also with a terrible sadness, as if someone close to me was suffering and I was feeling that suffering with them.

I am not given to premonitions and, so far as I was aware, no one close to me, no friend or family member, was in trouble. I felt quite well. The only thing that was in my mind was Theo Parmitter's strange story, but why should that have me, who had merely sat by the fire listening to it, so seized by fear? I felt weak and unwell so that I no longer wanted to be out tramping the streets alone and I turned sharply. There must have been a patch of frost exactly there for I felt my feet slither away from under me and fell heavily on the pavement. I lay winded and shaken but not in pain and it was at that moment that I heard, from a little distance away to my left, the cry and a couple of low voices. After that came the sound of a scuffle and then another desperate cry. It seemed to be coming from the direction of the Backs and yet, in some strange sense which is hard to explain, to be not *away* from me at all but here, at my hand, next to me. It is very difficult to convey a clear impression because nothing was clear, and I was also lying on a frozen pavement and anxious in case I had injured myself.

If what I had heard was someone being set upon in the dark and robbed – and that was as near to what it all sounded like as I could describe – then I should get up and either find the victim and go to his aid, or warn the policeman I had seen a few minutes before. Yet no one had been about. It was just after midnight, not a night for strollers, other than fools like me. It then came to me that I was in danger of being attacked myself. I had my wallet in my inner pocket, and a gold watch on my chain. I was worth a villain's attack. I pulled myself to my feet hastily. I was unhurt apart from a bash to the knee – I would be stiff the next day – and looked quickly round but there was no one about and no sound of footsteps. Had I imagined the noises? No, I had not. In a quiet street on a still and frosty night, when every sound carries, I could not have mistaken what I heard for wind in the trees, or in my own ears. I had heard a cry, and voices, and even a splash of water, yet although the sounds had come from the riverside, that was some distance away and hidden by the walls and gardens of the colleges.

I went back to the main thoroughfare and caught sight of the policeman again, trying the doorhandles of shops to check that they were secure. Should I go up to him and alert him that I had almost certainly heard a street robbery? But if I had heard the robbers, he, only a few yards away in a nearby street, must surely have heard them too, yet he was not rushing away but merely continuing down King's Parade with his steady, measured tread.

A car turned down from the direction of Trinity Street and glided past me. A cat streaked away into a dark slit between two buildings. My breath smoked on the frosty air. There was nothing untoward about and the town was settled for the night.

The oppression and dread that had enshrouded me a few minutes earlier had lifted, almost as a consequence of what I had heard and of my fall but I was puzzled and I did not feel comfortable in my own skin, and by now I was also thoroughly chilled so I made my way back to the college gate as briskly as I could, my coat collar turned up against the freezing night air.

The porter, still ensconced by his glowing fire, wished me goodnight. I replied, and turned into the court.

All was dark and quiet but light shone from one of the same two windows I had noticed when I went out, and now from another on the far left-hand row. Someone must just have returned. In a couple of weeks term would have begun and then lights would be on all round – undergraduates do not turn in early. I stood for a moment looking round, remembering the good years I had spent within these walls, the conversations late into the night, the japes, the hours spent sweating over an essay and boning up for Part One. I would never want to be like Theo, spending all my years here, however comfortable the college life might be, but I had a pang of longing for the freedoms and the friendships. It was then that my eye was caught by one light, the original one, going out, so that now there was only one room with a light on, on the far side, and it was automatic for me to glance up there.

What I saw made my blood freeze. Whereas before there had been a blank, now a figure was in the room and close to the window. The lamp was to one side of him and its beam was thrown onto his face, and the effect was startlingly like that of the Venetian picture. Well, there was nothing strange about that – lamplight and torchlight will always highlight and provide sharply contrasting shadows in this way. No, it was the face at the window by which I was transfixed. The man was looking directly at me and I could have sworn I recognized him, not from life but from the picture, because he bore such an uncanny resemblance to one of the faces that I would have sworn in any court that they were one and the same. But how could this possibly be? It could not, and besides, I had merely glanced at the one and it was at a window some distance from me, whereas the other was in a picture and I had studied it closely for some time. There are only so many combinations of features, as Theo himself had said.

But it was not the mere resemblance which struck so, it was the expression on the face at the window that had the impact upon me and produced such a violent reaction. The face was one I had particularly noticed in the picture because it was a fine depiction of decadence, of greed and depravity, of malice and loathing, of every sort of inhuman feeling and intent. The eyes were piercing and intense, the mouth full and sardonic, the whole face set into a sneer of arrogance and concupiscence. It was a mesmerizingly unpleasant face and it had repelled me in the picture as much as it horrified me now. I had glanced away, shocked, from the window, but now I looked up again. The face had gone and after another couple of seconds the light went out and the room was black. The whole court was now in darkness, save for the lamps at each corner, which cast a comforting pool of tallow light onto the gravel path.

I came to, feeling numb with cold and chilled with fear. I was shivering and the sense of dread and imminent doom had returned and seemed to wrap me round in place of my coat. But at the same time I was determined not to let these feelings get the better of me and I went across the court and up the staircase of the rooms from which the light had been shining. I remembered them as being the set a friend of mine had occupied in our time and found them without trouble. I stood outside the door and listened closely. There was a silence so absolute that it was uncanny. Old buildings generally make some sound, creaking and settling back, but here it was as still and quiet as the grave. After a moment, I knocked on the outer door, though without expecting any reply, as the occupant would now be in the bedroom and might well not have heard me. I knocked again more loudly, and when again there was no answer, I turned the door handle and stepped inside the small outer lobby. The air was bitterly cold here, which was strange as no one would be occupying rooms on such a night without having heated them. I hesitated, then went into the study.

'Hello,' I said in a low voice.

There was no response and after I had repeated my 'Hello' I felt along the wall for the light switch. The room was empty, and not only empty of any person, but empty of any thing, apart from a desk and chair, one armchair beside the cold and empty grate, and a bookcase without any books in it. There was an overhead light but no lamp of any kind. I went through to the bedroom. There was a bed, stripped of all linen. Nothing else.

Obviously, I had mistaken the rooms and I left, and made my way to the second set adjacent to them, the only others on the upper level of this staircase – each one had two sets up and a single, much larger set, on the ground floor and the pattern was the same on three sides of this, the Great Court. (The Inner Court was smaller and arranged quite differently.)

I knocked and, hearing only silence in response again, went into this set of rooms too. They were as empty as the first – emptier indeed since here there was no furniture other than the bookcases which were built into the wall. There was also a smell of plaster and paint.

I thought that I would go across to the night porter and ask who normally occupied this staircase. But what purpose would that serve? There were no undergraduates in residence, these sets had not been used by fellows for many years and clearly, decoration and maintenance were underway.

I cannot possibly have seen a lamp lit and a figure in any of these windows.

But I knew that I had.

I went, thoroughly shaken now, down the staircase, and across the court to the guest set in which I was staying. There, I had a bottle of whisky and a soda siphon. Ignoring the latter, I poured myself a large slug of the scotch and downed it in one, followed by another, which I took more slowly. I then went to bed and, in spite of the whisky, lay shivering for some time before falling into a heavy sleep. It was filled with the most appalling nightmares, through which I tossed and turned and sweated in horror, nightmares filled with strange flaring lights and fires and the shouts of people drowning.

I woke hearing myself cry out, and as I gathered my senses, I heard something else, a tremendous crash, as of something heavy falling. It was followed by a distant and muffled cry, as if someone had been hit and injured.

My heart was pounding so loudly in my ears and my brain still so swirling with the dreadful pictures that it took me a moment to separate nightmare from reality, but when I had been sitting upright with the lamp switched on for a few moments, I knew that what I had seen and the voices of the people drowning had been unreal and parts of a disturbing nightmare, but that the crashing sound and the subsequent cry most certainly had not. Everything was quiet now but I got out of bed and went into the sitting room. All was in order. I returned for my dressing gown, and then went out onto the staircase but here, too, all was still and silent. No one was occupying the adjacent set but I did not know if a fellow was in residence below. Theo Parmitter's rooms were on a different staircase.

I went down in the dark and icy cold and listened at the doors below but there was absolutely no sound.

'Is anyone there? Is everything all right?' I called but my voice echoed oddly up the stone stairwell and there was no answering call.

I went back to bed, and slept fitfully until morning, mainly because I was half frozen and found it difficult to get warm and comfortable again.

When I looked out of the windows a little after eight, I saw that a light snow had fallen and that the fountain in the centre of the court had frozen solid.

I was dressing when there was a hurried knock on the outer door and the college servant came in looking troubled.

'I thought you would want to know at once, sir, that there's been an accident. It's Mr Parmitter …'

FIVE

'THERE IS REALLY no need to trouble a doctor. I am a little shaken but unhurt. I will be perfectly all right.'

The servant had managed to get Theo into his chair in the sitting room, where I found him, looking pale and with an odd look about his eyes which I could not read.

'The doctor is on his way so there's an end to it,' I said, nodding approvingly at the servant, who had brought in a tray of tea and was refilling a water jug. 'Now tell me what happened.'

Theo leaned back and sighed, but I could tell that he was not going to argue further. 'You fell? You must have slipped on something. We must get the maintenance people to check ...'

'No. It is not their concern.' He spoke quite sharply.

I poured us both tea and waited until the servant had left. I had already noticed that the Venetian picture was no longer in its former place.

'Something happened,' I said. 'And you must tell me, Theo.'

He took up his cup and I noticed that his hand was shaking slightly.

'I did not sleep well,' he said at last. 'That is not unusual. But last night it was well after two before I got off and I slept very fitfully, with nightmares and general disturbance.'

'I had nightmares,' I said. 'Which is most unusual for me.'

'It is my fault. I should never have started on that wretched story.'

'Of course it is not — I went for a brisk walk to clear my head and woke myself up too thoroughly. It was also damned cold.'

'No. It was more than that, as it was with me. I am certain of it now. I was in such discomfort and sleeping so wretchedly that I knew I would be better off up and sitting in this chair. It takes me some time to get myself out of bed and stirring and I had heard the clock strike four when I made my way in here. As I came up to that wall on which the picture hung, I hesitated for a split second – something made me hesitate. The wire holding the painting snapped and the whole thing crashed down, glancing my shoulder so that I lost my balance and fell. If I had not paused, it would have hit me on the head. There is no question about it.'

'What made you pause? A premonition surely.'

'No, no. I daresay I was aware, subliminally, of the wire straining and being about to break. But the whole incident has shaken me a little.'

'I'm sorry – sorry for you, of course, but I confess I am sorry that I will not hear the rest of the story.'

Theo looked alarmed. 'Why? Of course, if you have to leave, or you prefer not to … but I wish that you would stay, Oliver. I wish that you would hear me out.'

'Of course I will. I could hardly bear to be left dangling like this but perhaps it would be better for your peace of mind if we let the whole thing drop.'

'Most emphatically it would not! If I do not tell you the rest I fear I shall never sleep well again. Now that it is buzzing in my mind it is as disturbing as a hive of angry bees. I must somehow lay them to rest. But do you now have to return to London?'

'I can stay another night — indeed it would be time well spent. There are some things I can usefully look at in the library while I am here.'

There was a tap on the door. The doctor arrived and I told Theo I would see him later that day, if he was up to talking — but that he must on no account disobey any 'doctor's orders' — the tale could wait. It was of no consequence. But I did not mean that. It was of more consequence now than I dared admit. Enough things had happened both to unnerve me and also to convince me that they were connected though each one taken alone meant little. I should say that I am by no means a man who jumps readily to outlandish conclusions. I am a scholar and I have been trained to require evidence, though as I am not a lawyer, circumstantial evidence will sometimes satisfy me well enough. I am also a man of strong nerve and sanguine temperament, so the fact that I had been disturbed by events is noteworthy. And I now knew that Theo Parmitter too was disturbed and, above all, that he had begun to tell me the story of the Venetian picture not to entertain me as we sat by the fire, but to unburden himself, to share his misgivings and fears with another human being, not unlike him in temperament, one who would bring a calm rational mind to bear upon them.

At least my mind, like my nervous state, had been calm until the previous night. Now, although my reason told me that the falling picture was a straightforward event and readily explained, my shadowy sense of foreboding and unease told me otherwise. I knew and often applied the principle of Occam's razor but, here, my intuition ruled my reason.

I spent most of the day in the library working on a medieval psalter and then went into the town to have tea in the Trumpington Street café I had often frequented and which was generally full of steam and the buzz of conversation. But that, of course, was in term-time. Now it was almost deserted and I sat eating my buttered crumpets in a somewhat chill and gloomy atmosphere. I had hoped to be cheered up by plenty of human company but even the shopping streets were quiet – it was too cold for strollers and anyone who had needed to buy something had done so speedily and returned to the warmth and snugness of home.

I would be doing the same tomorrow, and although I loved this town which had been of such benefit to me and in which I had spent some supremely happy years, I would not be sorry when this particular visit was over. It had been an unhappy and an unsettling one. I longed for the bustle of London and for my own comfortable house.

I returned to the college and, because I felt in need of company, went to dine in hall with half a dozen of the fellows. We made cheerful conversation and finished off a good bottle of port in the combination room in typical Cambridge fashion, so that it was rather late by the time I went across the court and up the staircase to my rooms. I found an anxious message awaiting me from Theo asking me to go and see him as soon as I was free.

I sat down for a few moments before doing so. I had, it was true, avoided going to see him since the morning, though I had of course enquired and been told that he was none the worse, physically, for the morning's incident, though still a little unnerved. I had managed to blow away the clinging cobwebs of my low and anxious mood and I was apprehensive about hearing any more of Theo's story. Yet he had all but begged me to go and hear him out, for his peace of mind depended upon it, and I felt badly about leaving him alone all day.

I hurried out and down the staircase.

❦

Theo was looking better. He had a small glass of malt whisky beside him, a good fire and a cheerful face and he enquired about my day in a perfectly easy manner.

'I'm sorry I was occupied and didn't get along here earlier.'

'My dear fellow, you're not in Cambridge to sit with me day and night.'

'All the same ...'

I sat down and accepted a glass of the Macallan. 'I have come to hear the rest of the story,' I said, 'if you feel up to it and still wish to tell me.'

Theo smiled.

The first thing I had looked for on coming into the room was the picture. It had been re-hung in its original position but it was in full shadow, the lamp turned away and shining on the opposite wall. I thought the change must have been made deliberately.

'What point had I reached?' Theo asked. 'I can't for the life of me remember.'

'Come, Theo,' I said quietly, 'I rather think that you remember very clearly, for all that you dropped off to sleep and I left you to your slumbers. You were coming to an important part of the story.'

'Perhaps my falling asleep was a gesture of self-defence.'

'At any rate, you need to tell me the rest or both of us will sleep badly again tonight. You had just shown me the article in the magazine, in which the picture appeared too prominently. I asked you if the photographer had placed it deliberately.'

'And he had not. So far as I was aware he had paid it no attention and I certainly had not done so. But there it was one might say dominating the photograph and the room. I was surprised but nothing more. And then, a couple of weeks after the magazine appeared, I received a letter. I have it still and I looked it out this morning. I had filed it away. It is there, on the table beside you.'

He pointed to a stiff, ivory-coloured envelope. I picked it up. It was addressed to him here in college and postmarked Yorkshire, some thirty years previously. It was written in violet ink and in an elaborate, old-style hand.

Hawdon
by Eskby
North Riding of Yorkshire

Dear Dr Parmitter,

I am writing to you on behalf of the Countess of Hawdon, who has seen an article about you and your work in the —Journal and wishes to make contact with you in regard to a painting in the room in which you appear photographed. The painting, an oil of a Venetian carnival scene, hangs immediately behind you and is of most particular and personal interest to her Ladyship.

Lady Hawdon has asked me to invite you here as there are matters to do with the picture that she needs most urgently to discuss.

The house is situated to the north of Eskby and a car will meet your train from the railway station at any time. Please communicate with me as to your willingness to visit her Ladyship and offer a date, at your convenience. I would stress again that because of her Ladyship's frail health and considerable agitation on this matter, an immediate visit would suit.

Yours etc
John Thurlby
Secretary.

'And did you go?' I asked, setting the letter down.

'Oh yes. Yes, I went to Yorkshire. Something in the tone of the letter meant that I felt I had no choice. Besides, I was intrigued. I was younger then and up for an adventure. I went off with a pretty light heart, as soon as term ended, within a couple of weeks.'

He leaned forward and poured himself another glass of whisky and indicated that I should do the same. I caught his expression in the light from the fire as he did so. He spoke lightly, of a jaunt to the north. But a haunted and troubled look had settled on his features that belied the conscious cheerfulness of his words.

'I do not know what I expected to find,' he said, after sipping his whisky. 'I had no preconceived ideas of the place called Hawdon or of this Countess. If I had ... You think mine is a strange story, Oliver. But my story is nothing, it is merely a prelude to the story told me by an extraordinary old woman.'

SIX

ORKSHIRE PROVED dismal and overcast on the day I made my journey. I changed trains in the early afternoon when rain had set in, and although the scenery through which we passed was clearly magnificent in decent weather, now I scarcely saw a hundred yards beyond the windows — no great hills and valleys and open moors were visible but merely lowering clouds over dun countryside. It was December, and dark by the time the slow train arrived, panting uphill, at Eskby station. A handful of other passengers got out and disappeared quickly into the darkness of the station passageway. The air was raw and a damp chill wind blew into my face as I came out into the forecourt, where two taxis and, at a little distance away, a large

black car were drawn up. The moment I emerged, a man in a tweed cap slid up to me through the murk.

'Dr Parmitter.' It was not a question. 'Harold, sir. I'm to take you to Hawby.'

Those were the only words he spoke voluntarily, the entire way, after he had put my bag in the boot and started up. He had automatically put me in the back seat, though I would have preferred to sit beside him, and as it was pitch dark once we had left the small town, which sat snugly on the side of a hill, it was a dreary journey.

'How much farther?' I asked at one point.

'Four mile.'

'Have you worked for Lady Hawdon many years?'

'I have.'

'I gather she is in poor health?'

'She is.'

I gave up, put my head back against the cold seat leather and waited, without saying any more, for the end of our journey.

What had I expected? A bleak and lonely house set

above a ravine, with ivy clinging to damp walls, a moat half empty, the sides slippery with green slime and the bottom black with stagnant water? An aged and skeletal butler, wizened and bent, and a shadowy, ravaged figure gliding past me on the stairs?

Well, the house was certainly isolated. We left the main country road and drove well over a mile, at a guess, over a rough single track but, at the end, it broadened out suddenly and I saw a gateway ahead with great iron gates standing open. The drive bent round so that at first there was only darkness ahead, but then we veered quite sharply to the right and over a low stone bridge, and peering through the darkness, I could see an imposing house with lights shining out from several of the high upper windows. We drew up on the gravel and I saw that the front door, at the top of a flight of stone steps, stood open. Light shone out from here too. It was altogether more welcoming than I had expected, and although a grand house it had a pleasing aspect and bore not the slightest resemblance to the House of Usher, whose fearsome situation I had been remembering.

I was greeted by a pleasant-faced butler, who introduced himself as Stephens, and taken up two flights of stairs to a splendid room whose long dark-red curtains were drawn against the dismal night and in which I found everything I could have wanted to pass a comfortable night. It was a little after six o'clock.

'Her Ladyship would like you to join her in the blue drawing room at seven thirty, sir. If you would ring the bell when you are ready I will escort you down.'

'Does Lady Hawdon dress for dinner?'

'Oh yes, sir.' The butler's face was impassive but I heard a frisson of disdain in his voice. 'If you do not have a dinner jacket ...'

'Yes, thank you, I do. But I thought it best to enquire.'

It had been only as an afterthought that I had packed the jacket and black tie, as I have always found it best to be over- rather than under-prepared. But I had now no idea at all what to expect from the evening ahead.

Stephens came promptly to lead me down the stairs and along a wide corridor, lined with many large oil paintings, some sporting prints, and cabinets full of curiosities, including masks, fossils and shells, silver and enamel. We walked too quickly for me to do more than glance eagerly from side to side but my spirits had lifted at the thought of what treasures there must be in the house and which I might be allowed to see.

'Dr Parmitter, m'Lady.'

It was an extremely grand room, with a magnificent fireplace, in front of which were three large sofas forming a group and on which lamplight and the light of the fire were focused. There were lamps elsewhere in the room, on small tables and illuminating pictures, but they were turned low. There were a number of fine paintings on the walls, Edwardian family portraits, hunting scenes, groups of small oils. At the far end of the room I saw a grand piano with a harpsichord nearby.

There was nothing decaying, dilapidated or chilling about such a drawing room. But the woman who sat on an upright chair with her face turned away from the fire did not match the room in warmth and welcome. She was extremely old, with the pale-parchment textured skin that goes with great age, a skin like the paper petals of dried

Honesty. Her hair was white and thin, but elaborately combed up onto her head and set with a couple of glittering ornaments. She wore a long frock of some green material on which a splendid diamond brooch was set, and there were diamonds about her long, sinewy neck. Her eyes were deep set but not the washed-out eyes of an old woman. They were a piercing, unnerving blue.

She did not move except to reach out her left hand to me, her eyes scrutinizing my face. I took the cold, bony fingers, which were heavily, even grotesquely jewelled, principally with diamonds again but also with a single large chunk of emerald.

'Dr Parmitter, please sit down. Thank you for coming here.'

As I sat, the butler appeared and offered champagne. I noticed that it was an extremely fine vintage and that the Countess was not drinking it.

'This is a very splendid house and you have some wonderful works of art,' I said.

She waved her hand slightly.

'I presume this is a family home of some generations?'

'It is.' There was a dreadful silence and I felt a miasma of gloom descend on me. This was going to be a tricky evening. The Countess was clearly not one for small talk, I still did not know exactly why I had been summoned, and in spite of the comfort and beauty surrounding me I felt awkward.

I wondered if we were to be alone for dinner.

Then she said, 'You cannot know what a shock I received on seeing the picture.'

'The Venetian picture? Your secretary mentioned in his letter to me ...'

'I know nothing of you. I do not customarily look at picture papers. It was Stephens who chanced upon it and naturally brought it to my attention. I was considerably shaken, as I say.'

'May I ask why? What the picture has to do with you – or perhaps with your family? Clearly it is of some importance for you to ask me here.'

'It is of more importance than I can say. Nothing else in life matters to me more. *Nothing else.*'

Her gaze held mine as a hand might hold another in a grip of steel. I could not look away and it was only the voice of the silent-footed butler, who now appeared behind us and announced dinner, which broke the dreadful spell.

The dining room was high-ceilinged and chill and we sat together at one end of the long table, with silver candlesticks before us and the full paraphernalia of china, silver and glassware as for an elaborate dinner. I wondered if the Countess sat in such state when she dined alone. I had offered her my arm across the polished floors into the dining room and it had been like having the claw of a bird resting there. Her back was bent and she had no flesh on her bones. I guessed that she must be well into her nineties. Sitting next to me, she seemed more like a moth than a bird, with the brilliant blue eyes glinting at me out of the pale skin, but I noticed that she was made up with rouge and powder and that her nails were painted. She had a high forehead behind which the hair was puffed out, and a beaky, bony nose, a thin line of mouth. Her cheekbones were high, too, and I thought that, with the blue of her eyes and with flesh on her distinguished bones, she might well have been a considerable beauty in her youth.

A plate of smoked fish was offered, together with thinly sliced bread and chunks of lemon, and a bowl of salad was set in front of us. I filled my mouth full, partly because I was hungry, but also in order not to have to talk for a few moments. A fine white Burgundy was poured, though, again, the

Countess drank nothing, save from the glass of water beside her. The dinner proceeded in a stately way and the Countess spoke little, save to give me some scraps of dullish information about the history of the house and estate and the surrounding area, and to ask me a couple of cursory questions about my own work. There was no liveliness at all in her manner. She ate little, broke up a piece of bread into small fragments and left them on her plate, and seemed tired and distant. I was gloomy at the thought of spending the rest of a long slow evening with her and frustrated that the point of my journey had not been reached.

At the end of dinner, the butler came to announce that coffee was served in the 'blue room'. The Countess took my arm and we followed him down the long corridor again and through a door into a small, wood-panelled room. I barely felt the weight of her hand but the fingers were pale bones resting on my jacket and the huge emerald ring looked like a carbuncle.

The blue room was partly a library, though I doubt if any of the heavy, leather-bound sets of books had been taken down from the shelves for years, and partly lined with dull maps of the county and legal documents with seals, framed behind glass. But there was a long polished table, on which were set out several large albums, and also the magazine with the article and the Venetian picture behind me, spread open. The butler poured coffee for me and a further glass of water for the Countess, helped her to a chair at the table before the books, and left us. As he did so, he turned the main lights down a little. Two lamps shone onto the table at either side of us and the Countess motioned for me to sit beside her.

She opened one of the albums, and I saw that it contained photographs, carefully placed and with names, places, dates, in neat ink. She turned several pages over carefully without explanation or inviting me to look, but at last came to a double spread of wedding photographs from seventy or more years ago, sepia pictures with the bridegroom seated, the bride standing, others with parents, the women draped in lace and wearing huge hats, the men moustached.

'My wedding, Dr Parmitter. Please look carefully.'

She turned the album round. I studied the various groups. The Countess had indeed been a very beautiful young woman, even as she stood unsmiling, as was the way in such photographs then, and I admired her long face with its clear skin, straight nose, small and pretty mouth, pert chin. Her eyes were large and deeply set and, even though these pictures were in sepia, I could imagine their astonishing blue.

'Does nothing strike you?'

It did not. I looked for a long time but knew no one, recognized nothing.

'Look at my husband.'

I did so. He was a dark-haired young man, the only male who was clean-shaven. His hair was slightly waved at the sides, his mouth rather full. He had a handsome face of character but not, I would say, rare character.

'I confess I do not know him – I recognize no one save yourself, of course.'

She turned her eyes on me now and her face wore a curious expression, partly of hauteur but also, I saw, of a distress I could not fathom.

'Please ...'

I glanced down again and, in that split second, had an extraordinary flash of – what? Shock? Recognition? Revelation?

Whatever it was, it must have shown clearly on my face, for the Countess said, 'Ah. Now you see.'

I was groping in the dark for a moment. I had seen and yet what had I seen? I now knew that there was something very familiar, I might almost say intimately familiar, about a face – but which face? Not hers, not that of ... No. His face. Her young husband's face. I knew it, or someone very like it. It was as though I knew it so well that it was the face of a member of my own family, a face I saw every day, a face with which I was so very familiar that I was, if you understand me, no longer aware of it.

Something was in the shadows of my mind, out of reach, out of my grasp, hovering but incomprehensible.

I shook my head.

'Look.' She had taken up the magazine and was gazing at it – for a moment, I thought she was gazing at the photograph of myself, sitting in my college rooms. But then she slid the paper across the table to me, one long thin finger pointing down.

There was a brief instant when what I saw made me experience a wave of shock so tremendous that I felt rising nausea and the room seemed to lurch crazily from side to side. What had been at the back of my mind came to the very front of it and clicked into place. Yet how could I believe what I was seeing? How could this be?

The Venetian picture was very clear in the magazine photograph, but even if it had not been, I knew it so well, so thoroughly and intimately, I was so familiar with every detail of it, that I could not have been mistaken. There was, you remember, one particular scene within the scene. A young man was being held by the arm and threatened by another person, on the point of stepping into one of the boats, and his head was turned to look into the eyes of whoever was viewing the picture, with an expression of strange, desperate terror and of pleading. Now, I looked at it and it was vivid, even at one stage removed, through a photograph. The face of the young man being persuaded into the boat was the face of the Countess's husband. There was no doubt about it. The resemblance was absolute. This was not a near-likeness. The two young men did not share a similar physiognomy. They were one and the same. I saw it in the eyes, on the lips, in the set of the forehead, the jut of the jaw. Everything came together in a moment of recognition.

She was staring at me intently.

'My God,' I whispered. But I struggled for words, tried to grab hold of sanity. There was, of course, a sensible, an ordinary, a rational explanation.

'So your husband was a sitter for the artist.' As I said it, I knew how ridiculous it was.

'The picture was painted in the late eighteenth century.'

'Then – this is a relative? One you perhaps have only just discovered? This is an extraordinary family likeness.'

'No. It is my husband. It is Lawrence.'

'Then I do not understand.'

She was leaning over the photograph now, gazing at the picture and at the face of her young husband, with an intensity of longing and distress such as I had never seen.

I waited for some time. Then she said, 'I would like to return to the drawing room. Now that you have seen this, now that you know ... I can tell you what there is to tell.'

'I would like to hear it. But I have no idea how I can help you.'

She put out her hand for me to assist her up.

'We can make our own way. We have no need of Stephens.'

Once more, the thin, weightless hand rested on my arm and we walked the length of the corridor, now in shadow as the wall lamps had been dimmed, so that the pictures and cabinets receded into darkness except when the gilt corner of a frame or a panel of glass glowed eerily in the tallow light.

THE COUNTESS'S STORY

WAS MARRIED when I was twenty. I met my husband at a ball and we experienced a *coup de foudre*. Few people are lucky enough to know that thing commonly called love at first sight. Few people really know and understand its utterly transforming power. We are the fortunate ones. Such an experience changes one entirely and for ever.

It was such an ordinary place to meet. That is how young people all met one another in those days, is it not? I daresay they still do. But how many of them know such instant, such blinding love? He was several years older, in his early thirties. But that did not matter. Nothing mattered. My parents were a little concerned – I was young, and I had an elder sister who should, in the natural order of these things, have been married before me. But they looked upon Lawrence with favour, nevertheless. There was only one thing to trouble us. He had been on the verge of an engagement. He had not proposed but there was an understanding. If he and I had not met that evening, it is sure that there would have been an engagement and a marriage and naturally the young woman in question was bitterly hurt. These things happen, Dr Parmitter. I had no reason to feel in any way to blame. Nor, perhaps, had he. But of course he felt a great concern for the girl and I – when I was eventually told – I felt as great a guilt and sorrow as a girl of twenty in the throes of such a love could be expected to feel. What happens in these cases? What usually happens is that one party suffers for a certain period of time from hurt pride and a broken heart, both of which are eventually healed, generally by the arrival of another suitor.

In this instance, it was otherwise. The young woman, whose name was Clarissa Vigo, suffered so greatly that I believe it turned her mind. I had not known her at all prior to this but I had been assured, and had no reason to doubt it, that she had been a charming, gentle, generous young woman. She became a bitter, angry, tormented one whose only thought was of the injury she had suffered and how she could obtain revenge. Of course, the best way was to destroy our happiness. That is what she set her mind to and what consumed her time and energy and passion. Much of this was kept from me, at least at first, but I learned afterwards that her family despaired of her sanity to the extent that they had her visited by a priest!

This was not the parish vicar, Dr Parmitter. This was a priest who undertook exorcisms. He was called both to houses under the influence of unhappy spirits and to persons behaving as if they were possessed. I believe that is how the young woman was treated. But he came away, he said, in despair. He felt unable to help her because she would not allow herself to be helped. Her bitterness and desire for retribution had become so strong that they possessed her entirely. They became her reason for living. Whether that is what you would class as demonic possession I do not know. I do know that she set out to destroy. And she succeeded. She succeeded in the most terrible way. I have always believed that if the priest could have exorcised her demons then, all would have been well, but as he could not things grew worse, her determination grew stronger and with it her power to do harm. She was indeed possessed. Anger and jealousy are terrible forces when united together with an iron will.

But to begin with I was unaware of any of this. Lawrence referred only briefly and somewhat obliquely to her, and of course I was obsessed and possessed in my turn – by an equally single-minded and powerful love.

My time and energies were entirely consumed by Lawrence and by our forthcoming marriage, preparations for our new home and so forth. All that is perfectly usual of course. I was not an unusual young woman, you know. Two things happened in the weeks before our marriage. I received an anonymous letter.

Anonymous? It was unsigned and I did not know who had sent it. Not then. It was full of poison. Poison against me, against Lawrence, bitter, vindictive poison. It contained a threat, too, to destroy our future. To bring about pain and shock and devastating loss. I was terrified by it. I had never known hatred in my happy young life and here it was, directed at me, hatred and the desire – no, more, the determination to harm. For several days I kept the letter locked in a drawer of my writing desk. It seemed to sear through the wood. I seemed to smell it, to feel the hatred that emanated from it, every time I went near, so that in the end I tore it into shreds and burned it in the hearth. After that I tried to put it out of my mind.

We were to be married the following month and naturally wedding presents began to arrive at my parents' house – silver, china and so forth – and I was happily occupied in unpacking and looking at it all, and in writing little notes of thanks. And one day – I remember it very clearly – along with some handsome antique tables and a footstool, a picture arrived. There was a card with it, on which was written the name of the painter, and a date, 1797. There was also a message To the Bride and Bridegroom. Let what is begun be completed in the same hand as the malign letter.

I hated the picture from the moment I first saw it. Partly, of course, that was because it came from someone unknown, the same someone who had sent me the letter and who wished us harm. But it was more than that. I did not know much about art but I had grown up among delightful pictures which had come down through my family on my mother's side, charming English pastoral scenes and paintings of families with horses and dogs, still-life oils of flowers and fruit, innocent, happy things which pleased me. This was a dark, sinister painting in my eyes. If I had known the words 'corrupt' and 'decadent' then I would have used them to describe it. As I looked at the faces of those people, at the eyes behind the masks and the strange smiles, the suggestions of figures in windows, figures in shadows, I shuddered. I felt uneasy, I felt afraid.

But when Lawrence saw the picture he had nothing but praise for it. He found it interesting. When he asked me who had sent it I lied. I said that I had mislaid the card, muddled it with others in so much unwrapping. I could certainly not have expressed to him any of my feelings about the picture – they were so odd, even to me, so unlike anything I had ever experienced. I could not have found the right words for them and, in any case, I would have been afraid of being ridiculed. Two secrets. Not a good way to begin a marriage, you may feel. But what else should I have done?

I had had so little experience of the world and of different kinds of people. I had led a happy and a sheltered upbringing. So it was not until a day or two before our wedding that I understood who had sent both the anonymous letter and the picture, and then only when I chanced to see an envelope addressed to Lawrence in the same handwriting. I asked him who had sent it and he told me, of course, that it was from the young woman he might have married. I remember his tone of voice, as if he were holding something back from me, as if he were trying not to make anything of the letter. It was just some snippet of information he had asked for many months before, he said, and changed the subject. I was not worried that he had any feelings for her. I was worried because I knew at once that he, too, had received a letter full of hatred and ill-will, that he wanted to protect me and keep it from me, that the woman was the sender of the picture. I did not ask him. I did not need to ask him. But once all of these things fell into place, I was more than ever afraid. Yet of what I was afraid – how could I know? I disliked the picture – it repelled me, made me shudder. But it was just a picture. We could hang it in some distant corner of our house, or even leave it wrapped and put it away.

Our wedding was a happy occasion, of course. Everyone was happy – our families, our friends. We were happy. Only one person in the world was not but naturally she did not attend and on that day no one could have been further from our thoughts.

I did as best I could to put the incidents and the painting out of my mind and we began our married life. Six weeks after the wedding, Lawrence's father, the Earl of Hawdon, died very suddenly. Lawrence was the eldest son and I found myself, not yet even twenty-one years old, the mistress of this large house and with a husband thrust into the running of a huge estate. We had taken a short honeymoon on the south coast and planned a longer tour the following spring. Now, perhaps we would never undertake it.

I have said that my father-in-law died suddenly — quite suddenly and unexpectedly. He had been in the best of health — he was an energetic man, and he was found dead at his desk one evening after dinner. A stroke. Of course we believed the medical men. One must. What reason was there to doubt them?

I have now to tell you something which I expect you to disbelieve. At first, that is to say, you will disbelieve it. I would ask you to go across to the bureau in the far corner of this room and look at the framed photograph which stands there.

I crossed the long, silent room, leaving the Countess, a tiny, wraithlike figure hunched into her chair in the circle of lamplight, and entering the shadows. But there was a lamp on the bureau, which I switched on. As I did so, I caught my breath.

I saw a photograph in a plain silver frame. It was of a man in middle age, sitting at this same desk and half turning to the camera. His hands rested on the blotter which was in front of me now. He had a high forehead, a thick head of hair, a full mouth, heavy lids. It was a good face, a strong, resolute face of character, and a handsome one too. But I was transfixed by the face because I knew it. I had seen it before, many times. I was familiar with it.

I had lived with that face.

I looked back to the old woman sitting once again with her head back, eyes closed, a husk.

But she said, her voice making me start, 'So now you see.'

My throat was dry and I had to clear it a couple of times before I could answer her, and even when I did so, my own voice sounded strange and unfamiliar.

'I see but I scarcely know what it is that I do see.'

But I did know. Even as I spoke, of course I

knew. I had known the instant I set eyes on the photograph. And yet … I did not understand.

I returned to my chair opposite the old woman.

'Please refill your glass.'

I did so thankfully. After I had downed my whisky and poured a second, I said, 'Now, I confess I do not understand but I can only suppose this is some hoax ... the painting cannot be of its date, of course, there is some trick, some faking? I hope you will explain.'

I had spoken in a falsely amused and over-loud tone and as the words dropped into the silent space between us, I felt foolish. Whatever the explanation, it was not a matter for jest.

The Countess looked at me with disdain.

'There is no question of either a hoax or a mistake. But you know it.'

'I know it.'

Silence. I wondered how this great house could be so silent. In my experience old houses are never so, they speak, they have movements and soft voices and odd footfalls, they have a life of their own, but this house had none.

Nothing happened immediately. My father-in-law was dead and we were thrown into the usual business which surrounds a death – and my husband found himself pitched into a wholly new life with all its responsibilities. We had not even moved into the small house at the far side of the estate which was to have been our married home, and now we found ourselves forced to take over this house instead. We had barely unpacked our wedding presents and there was no place for most of them here. It was a week after we had moved in. Lawrence and his mother of course were shocked and still in deep mourning. I was sad but I had known my father-in-law so little. I wandered about this great place like a lost soul, trying to get to know each room, to find a role for myself, to keep out of everyone's way. It was on these wanderings that I finally came upon the Venetian picture. It had been put with some other items into one of the small sitting rooms on the first floor – a room that I think was rarely used. It smelled of damp and had an empty, purposeless air. The curtains hung heavy, the furniture seemed ill-chosen.

The picture was propped up on a half-empty bookcase. It faced me as I went into the room. And ... and it seemed to me that it drew me to it and that every face within it looked into mine. I cannot describe it better. Every face. I wanted to leave the room at once, but I could not, the picture drew me to itself as if every person painted there had the strength to reach out and pull me towards it. As I approached it, some of the faces receded, some disappeared completely into the shadows and were no longer there after all. But one face was there. It was a face at a window. There is a palazzo with two lighted windows and with open shutters and a balcony overlooking the Grand Canal. In one of those lighted rooms, but looking out as if desperate to escape, even to fling himself over the balcony into the waters below to get away, there was a man, turned towards me. His body was not clearly depicted – his clothes seem to be only sketched in hastily, almost as an afterthought. But his face ... It was the face of my father-in-law, so lately, so suddenly dead. It was his exact likeness save that it wore an expression I had never seen him wear, one full of fear and desperation, of panic. Horror? Yes, even horror. I knew that I had not only never noticed his face, his likeness, in the picture before but that, absolutely and unmistakably, *it had not been there.*

You can imagine that scene, Dr Parmitter. I was a very young woman who had already been subjected to a number of great changes in my life. I had encountered passionate and single-minded hatred and jealousy for the first time, come face to face with sudden death for the first time, and now I was alone in a remote room of this house which was home and yet could not have felt less like a home to me, and looking into the terrified face of my dead father-in-law trapped inside a picture.

I felt nauseous and faint and I remember grabbing hold of a chair and holding on to it while the ground dipped and swayed beneath me. I was' terrified and bewildered. What should I do? Who could I speak to about this? How could I bring my husband here to see the picture? How could I begin to tell him what I had so far kept entirely to myself? Only two people knew anything of this – I myself and the woman, Clarrisa Vigo. I was faced with something I did not understand and was poorly equipped to deal with.

I dared not touch the picture, or I would have taken it down and turned it face to the wall, or carried it up to one of the farthest attics and hidden it there. But I doubted if many people came into this fusty little room. On leaving it, I discovered that the key was in the lock, so I turned it and put the key in my pocket. Later, I slipped it into a drawer of my dressing table.

The following weeks were too busy and too exhausting, too strange, for me to think much about the picture, though I had nightmares about it and I preferred not to go down the corridor leading to the small sitting room but would always take a long detour. My mother-in-law was in mourning and great distress and

I had to spend much time with her, as of course Lawrence was occupied from dawn till dusk in taking up the reins of the estate. She was a kindly but not very communicative woman and my memories of this time are mainly of sitting in this drawing room or in her own small boudoir, turning the pages of a book which I never managed to read, or glancing through country magazines, while she sat with crochet on her lap, her hands still, staring ahead of her. And I carried a dreadful and bewildering secret within me, knowledge I did not want and could not share. I had never before quite understood that once a thing is known it cannot be unknown. Now I did. Oh, I did.

I became even thinner and Lawrence once or twice commented that I looked pale or tired. He came to me one day saying that he wanted us to get away, though it could only be for a week or ten days at most, and that we would travel down through France and Italy by train to Venice. He was so pleased, so anxious for me to be well and happy. I should have welcomed it all. We had barely spent any time alone together and I had never travelled. But when he told me that we were to visit Venice I felt a terrible sensation, as if someone's hand had squeezed my heart so tightly that for a moment I could not breathe.

But there was nothing I dared say, nothing I could do. I had to endure in silence.

One thing happened before we left. We were invited to a very large dinner at the house of a neighbour in the county, and as we were seated, I looked up to see that opposite me, exactly opposite, so that I could not avoid her gaze, was Clarissa Vigo. I do not think I have said that she was a remarkably beautiful woman and she was also beautifully dressed. I was not clever at dressing. I wore simple clothes, which Lawrence always preferred, and did not like to stand out. Clarissa stood out and I sat across the table feeling both inferior and afraid. Her eyes kept finding me out, looking over the silver and the flowers, challenging me to meet her gaze. When I did it made me tremble. I have never known such hatred, such malevolence. I tried to ignore it, to talk to my neighbours and bend my head to my plate, but she was there, watching, filled with loathing and a terrible sort of power. She knew. She knew that she had power over me, over us. I felt ill that evening, ill with fear.

But it passed. She did not speak a word to me. It was over.

A week later, we left for our trip to Europe.

I will not take you step by step with us down through France and the northern part of Italy. We were happy, we were together, and the strains and responsibilities of the past months receded. We could pretend to be a carefree, recently married couple. But a dark shadow hung over me, and even as I was happy, I dreaded our arrival in Venice. I did not know what would or could happen. Many times, I told myself severely that my fears were groundless and that Clarissa Vigo had no power, no power over either of us.

Dr Parmitter, I have read that everyone who visits Venice falls in love with that city, that Venice puts everyone under her spell. Perhaps I was never going to be happy there, because of the painting and of what I had seen, but I was taken aback by how much I disliked it from the moment we arrived. I marvelled at the buildings, the canals, and the lagoon astonished me. And yet I hated it. I feared it. It seemed to be a city of corruption and excess, an artificial place, full of darkness and foul odours. I looked over my shoulder. I saw everything as sinister and threatening and, as I did so, I knew that an unbridgeable chasm had opened between Lawrence and myself, for he loved the city, adored it, said he was never happier.

I could only follow him and smile and remain silent. It was a hard, a bitter week, the days passed so slowly, and all the time, I was in a state of dread. I felt isolated within an invisible cell, where I suffered and feared and could only wait, helplessly. My love for my dear husband had turned to a terrible thing, a desperation, a passionate, fearful clinging desire to possess and hold and keep. I did not want to let him out of my sight, and when he was within it, I looked and looked at him in case I forgot him. How strange that must sound. But it is true. I was possessed by fear and dread.

We were to be there for five nights and the blow fell on the third. I fell asleep in the afternoon. I found Venice enervating and my fear exhausting. I could not help myself and while I slept Lawrence went out. He liked simply to wander in and out of the squares and over the bridges, looking, enjoying. When I woke he was in the room and smiling with delight. He had bumped into friends, he said, I would never believe it, except that one always did meet everyone one knew in Venice. They lived here for several months of the year, and had a palazzo on the Grand Canal. Tomorrow night, there was a mini-Carnival, with a masked ball. They were to go, they would be taking a party. We were to join them. Costumiers would be visited, costumes and masks hired, he had arranged an appointment in an hour's time.

How can I convey to you the fearfulness of that place? It was a narrow dark shop in one of the innumerable alleyways and reached a long way back. The walls were festooned with costumes, masks and hats, all of them, I was told, traditional to carnivals and balls in Venice for hundreds of years and none of them to me pretty or beautiful or fun, every one sinister and strange. One could dress as a weeping Jew, a satyr, a butcher, a king with his sceptre or a man with a monkey on his shoulder; as a peasant girl with a baby, a street ruffian or a masquerader on stilts; as Pantaloon, Pulcinello, or the plague doctor. As a woman I had less choice and Lawrence wanted me to wear silk and lace and taffeta with an ornate jewelled mask, but I preferred to go as the peasant girl with her child in a basket: I could not have borne to dress up any more elaborately, though I was still obliged to take a mask on its ribboned stick. Lawrence hired a great black cloak and tricorn hat, and his mask was black and covered in mother of pearl buttons. He had long shining boots too. He was thrilled, excited, he was like a child going off to a party. I could not bear to see him and by now I was in a fever of dread. I could not prevent my bouts of sudden trembling and I saw that my face was deathly pale. I prayed for the whole thing to come and go quickly, because I somehow felt sure that when it had gone, so would whatever it was that I feared be gone too.

It was a hot night and I was nauseated by the smell of the foetid canals, whose slimy black water seemed to me full of all the filth and scum of the city. There were the smells of oil and smoke from the flares, and from street food vendors, smells of hot charred meat and peculiar spices. The ballroom of the palazzo was packed with people and noise and I found it strange and sinister not being able to see faces, not to know if people were old or young or even man or woman. But there was good food and drink to which one helped oneself and I revived myself by eating fruit and sweetmeats and drinking some sparkling wine, and then I danced with Lawrence and the evening seemed, if not very pleasurable, at least less frightening than I had feared. The time passed.

I was almost enjoying myself, almost relaxed, when it was announced that we were to leave the palazzo and go down into the streets, to parade through the squares to the light of flares, watched by the citizens from all their windows, joined by passers-by – the whole celebration would move out to become part of the city. Apparently this was usual. The people expected it. There was then a great exodus, a rush and general confusion, during which I became separated from my husband. I found myself pushed along among the other revellers, beside a Pulcinello and a priest and a wicked old witch, as we crowded down the great staircase and streamed outside. The torches were flaring. I can see them now, orange and smoking against the night sky. You can see the scene, Dr Parmitter. You have seen it often enough. The light glancing on the dark waters. The waiting gondolas. The crowds pressing forward. The masks. The eyes gleaming. The lights in the other buildings along the Grand Canal. You have seen it all.

What happened next I can barely believe or bring myself to tell. You may dismiss it. Any sane person would. I would not believe it. I do not believe it. But I know it to be true.

We were outside the Palazzo on the landing stage. Some of the crowd had already gone on into the streets on that side of the canal – we could hear the laughter and the cries. People were leaning out of windows now, looking down on us all. The gondolas were lining up waiting to take us out onto the canal, over to the other side, up to the Rialto Bridge … occasionally they bumped together and rocked and the reflection of their lamps also rocked wildly, sickeningly, in the churning water. I was standing a yard or two from Lawrence when suddenly I heard my name called. Of course, I turned my head. The strange thing was that I responded even though it was my old name I heard, my maiden name. Who here knew my former name? The voice had come from behind me, but when I looked round I saw no one I knew — not everyone was still masked, but every face was strange in one way or another. And then I thought I saw not a face, but only the eyes, of someone I recognized. They were the eyes of Clarissa Vigo, looking out from a white silk mask with silver beads below a great plume of white feathers. How could I know? I knew.

I tried to move through the throng on the landing stage to get closer to her, but someone swung towards me and I had to avoid them or I would have been knocked over. When I looked again the white-masked woman had gone.

The gondoliers were crying out and the water was splashing over the wooden stage and someone was trying to get me to go on board. I would not go alone, of course, I wanted only to go if my husband would too – and indeed, I would infinitely have preferred not to embark on one of the gondolas and slink off across that dark and sinister water. I drew back and then I started to look for Lawrence. I searched for him there, and then I made my way down the side of the building and over the narrow bridge which led into a square. But the revellers had moved far on, I could not even hear them now, and the cobbled square was in almost total darkness. I retreated and now there was panic in my search. Lawrence was not on the landing stage and I was as certain as I could be that he would never have crossed the canal without me. I thought I should return inside the palazzo and look for him there. I was frightened. I had seen the woman, I had heard her whisper my name. I had dreaded this night, this place, and now I was dry-mouthed with fear.

But as I tried to make my way to the open

doors of the palazzo, I heard a commotion behind me and then a shout. It was my husband who was shouting to me but I had never heard his voice sound like it. He was shouting in alarm – no, in terror, in horrible fear. I pushed forward and managed to reach the edge of the wooden landing stage. The last gondola laden with revellers was pulling away and I searched it in vain for a glimpse of my husband but there was no one like him or dressed like him. Most of the people had gone. A few stood, apparently uncertain if another gondola would come up and unable to decide if they wanted to go aboard if it did. I went back into the palazzo. The great rooms were deserted apart from some servants who were clearing the last of the feast. I spoke no Italian, but I asked if they had seen my husband and went on asking. They smiled, or gestured, but did not understand. Everyone else had gone. I found my cape and left. I ran through the squares, into the main piazza, ran like a mad demented creature, calling Lawrence's name. No one was about. A beggar was lying in an alleyway and snarled at me, a dog barked and snapped as I ran past. I reached our hotel in a state of frenzy yet I was sure there might still be an innocent explanation, that Lawrence would be there, waiting. But he was not. I roused the entire hotel, and was in such distress that after pressing a glass of brandy to my lips, the proprietor called the police.

Lawrence was never found. I stayed on in Venice for sixteen days beyond the original date for our departure. The police search could hardly have been more thorough but nothing came to light. No one had seen him, no one else had heard his voice that last time. No one remembered anything. It was concluded that he had accidentally slipped into the canal and drowned but his body was never discovered. He was not washed up. He had simply vanished.

I returned home. Home? This great hollow barren place? But yes, it was my home.

I was in such a state of distress that I fell ill and for two or three weeks the doctors feared for my life. I remember almost nothing of that terrible time but sometimes, in the midst of feverish dreams, I heard my husband crying out, sometimes I felt that he was just beside me, that if I reached out my hand I could save him. All through this time, something would slide towards my conscious mind but then dodge out of my grasp, as happens when a particular name eludes one. Through feverish days and the storms of my nightmares, it was there, just out of reach, this piece of information, this knowledge – I did not even know what it was.

I recovered slowly. I was able to sit up in a chair, then to be taken into the garden room to benefit from the sunshine during the afternoon. I asked time and time again for news of Lawrence but there never was any. My mother-in-law, who had received a double blow in such a few months, was sunk into a profound, silent depression and I barely saw her.

And then I discovered, as I was beginning to feel stronger, that I was expecting a child. My husband was the last of the line and the title would have died out with his death – if indeed he were dead. Now, and if I had a son, title, estates, house, would be secure. I had a reason to live. My mother-in-law rallied too.

The nightmares loosened their hold and

became strange dreams with only intermittent horrors. But in the middle of one night I woke suddenly, because what had been hovering just out of reach had come cleanly into my mind. It was not a thought or a name, it was an image, and as I recognized it, I felt icy cold. My hands were stiff so that I could hardly move my fingers but I managed to get into my dressing robe, to find the key in my dressing table and to leave my bedroom, and make my way slowly down the long, dark, silent corridors of the house. The portraits and the sporting prints seemed to loom towards me. The cabinets of artifacts – there are endless collections in this place – gleamed in the light of the small torch I had brought, for I did not want to switch on any lights and, indeed, did not know where half of the switches might be found. Odd shapes, stones and dead birds and moths and bits of bronze, pieces of bone, feathers, even tiny skulls – Lawrence's family had been travellers, collectors and hoarders, everything came back here to Hawdon and was found a place. I wondered fleetingly how a tiny child would view these old, musty, hideous things. The further I walked down through this little-used end of the house, the stronger was the image in my mind. I felt ill, I felt weak, I felt afraid yet I had no choice but to see this dreadful thing through. If I did so, perhaps I would rid myself of the horrible image once and for all.

There were no sounds at all. My slippered feet barely seemed to make any impression on the long runner of carpet down the middle of the corridor. I had a sensation of being watched and not so much followed as accompanied, as if someone were close to my side the whole way, making sure I did not weaken and turn back. Oh it was a dreadful journey. I shudder when I remember it, as I often, so often, do.

I reached the door of the small sitting room and turned the key. It smelled of old furniture and fabrics which had been sealed in against any fresh air and light. But I did not want to be here with only my torch, and when I found the switch, the two lamps, with their thin light, came on and then I saw the picture again. And as I saw it, I realized that in the mustiness I could smell something else, a hint of something sharp and very distinctive. It took me a second or two to work out that it was paint, fresh oil paint. I looked around everywhere. Perhaps this room was used after all, perhaps one of the servants had been here to repair or repaint something, though I could see no sign of it. Nor were there any painting materials or brushes lying about.

The picture was as I had left it, with its face to the wall, and once I had located it I stood for long moments, hearing my heart pound in my ears and shaking with fear. But I knew that I would never rest until I had satisfied myself that I was in the grip of fancies and nightmares, caused by the shocks, distress and illness I had suffered.

In a single moment of determination, I took hold of the painting, turned it, and then looked at it with wide-open eyes.

At first, it seemed exactly as before. It reminded me starkly of that horrible evening and of the masks and costumes, the noise, the smell, the light from the torches and of losing my husband among the crowd. Some of the costumes and masks were familiar but, of course, they are traditional, they have been on display on such occasions in Venice for hundreds of years.

And then I saw. First, I saw, in one corner, almost hidden in the crowd, the head of someone wearing a white silk mask and with white plumes in the hair and the eyes of Clarissa Vigo. It was the eyes that convinced me I was not imagining anything. They were the same staring, brilliant, malevolent eyes, wishing me harm, full of hatred but also now with a dreadful gloating in them. They seemed to be both looking straight at me, into me almost, and to be directing me elsewhere. How could eyes look in two places at once, at me and at ...

I followed them. I saw.

Standing up at the back of a gondola was a man wearing a black cloak and a tricorn hat. He was between two other heavily masked figures. One had a hand on his arm, the other was somehow propelling him forwards. The black water was choppy beneath the slightly rocking gondola. The man had his head turned to me. The expression on his face was ghastly to see —

it was one of abject terror and of desperate pleading. He was trying to get away. He was asking to be saved. He did not want to be on the gondola, in the clutches of those others.

It was unmistakably a picture of my husband and the last time I had seen the Venetian painting, *it had not been there* – of that I was as sure as I was of my own self. My husband had become someone in a picture painted two hundred years before. I touched the canvas with one finger but it was clean and dry. There was no sign that anything had been painted onto it or changed at all within it at any recent time, and in any case, I could no longer smell the oil paint that had been so pungent moments before.

I was faint with shock and distress, so that I was forced to sit down in that dim little room. I could not explain what had happened or how but I knew that an evil force had caused it and knew who was responsible. Yet it made no sense. It still makes no sense.

One thing I did know, and it was with a certain relief, was that Lawrence was dead – however, wherever, in whatever way dead, whether 'buried alive' in this picture or buried in the Grand Canal, he was dead. Until now I had hoped against hope that one day I would receive a message telling me that he had been found alive. Now I knew that no such message could ever come.

I remember little more. I must have made my way back to my room and slept, but the next day I woke to the picture before my eyes again and I made myself go back to look at it. Nothing had changed. In such daylight as filtered between the heavy curtains and half-barred windows of the sitting room, which overlooked an inner courtyard, I saw the painting where I had left it and the face of my husband looking out at me, beseeching me to help him.

She was silent for a long time. I think she had exhausted herself. We sat on opposite one another not speaking, but I felt a closeness of understanding and I wanted to tell her of my own small experiences in the presence of the Venetian picture, of how it often troubled me.

I was wondering if I should simply get up and make my way to my room, leaving any further conversation until the following day when she would be more refreshed, but then the blue eyes were open and on my face as the Countess said, 'I must have that picture,' in such a fierce and desperate tone, that I started.

'I do not understand,' I replied, 'how it left your hands and eventually came into mine.'

Her old face crumpled and tears came then, softening the glare of those brilliant blue eyes.

'I am tired,' she said. 'I must ask you to wait until tomorrow. I do not think I have the strength to tell you any more of this terrible story tonight. But I am spurred on by the thought that it will soon be over and I will be able to rest. It has been a long, long search, an apparently hopeless journey but now it is almost at an end. It can wait a few more hours.'

I was unsure exactly what she meant but I agreed that she should rest as long as she wished and that I was at her disposal at any time the next day. She asked me to ring the bell for Stephens, who appeared at once to show me to my room. I took her hand for a moment as she sat, like a little bird, deep in the great chair, and, on a strange impulse, lifted it to my lips. It was like kissing a feather.

I slept badly. The wind blew, rattling the catches every so often, and episodes of the strange story the Countess had told me came back to me and I tried hopelessly to work out some rational explanation for it all. I would have dismissed her as old and with a failing mind had it not been for my own experiences with the picture. I was uneasy in that house and her story had disturbed me profoundly. I knew only too well the fierce power of jealousy which fuels a passion to be avenged. It does not happen very often but when it does and a person has their love rejected and all their future hopes betrayed for another, rage, pride and jealousy are terrible forces and can do immeasurable harm. Who knows that they could not do even these evil supernatural deeds?

But my own part in all of this was innocent. I had nothing to fear from the jilted woman who in any case was presumably long dead, or, I imagined, from the Countess. Yet as I lay tossing and turning through that long night, it seemed as if I was indeed being possessed by something unusual – for there grew in me an absolute determination to keep the Venetian picture. Why I should now so desperately want it, I did not know. It was of value but not priceless. It had caused me some trouble and anxiety. I did not need it. But just as, when I had been approached by the sweating, breathless man after the sale, desperate that I sell it to him for any amount of money I cared to name, I again felt a stubbornness I had never known. I would not sell then, and I would neither sell nor give back the painting to the Countess now. I felt almost frightened of my resolution, which made no sense and which seemed to have taken hold of me by dint of some outside force. For of course she had brought me here to ask for the painting. What other reason could there be? She could not have simply wanted to tell her story to a stranger.

I did not see her until late the following morning and occupied myself by taking a long walk around the very fine parkland and then by enjoying the excellent and I thought little-used library. I met no one other than a few groundsmen and maids cleaning the house and the latter scurried away like mice into holes on seeing me. But a little after eleven the silken-footed Stephens materialized and told me that coffee and the Countess awaited me in the morning room.

He led me there. It was a delightful room, furnished in spring yellows and light greens and with long windows onto the gardens, through which the sun was now shining. It is extraordinary how a little sunshine and brightness will lift both the aspect of any room, and of one's spirits on entering it. My tiredness and staleness from the sleepless night lifted and I was glad to see the old Countess, looking still small and frail but with rather more colour and liveliness than by the light of evening lamps.

I began to make remarks about the grounds and so on but she cut me short.

There is only a little more to tell. I will complete the story.

I gave birth to a son, Henry. This family has always alternated the names of the male heirs – Lawrence and Henry, for many generations.

All was well. I kept the door of the small sitting room locked and the key in its turn locked in my dressing table and from that first terrible night I did not go into it again.

My mother-in-law lived here and my son grew up. Gradually, I became used to my state and to this house as being my home – and naturally I adored my only son, who looked so very like his father.

At his coming-of-age, we gave a great party – neighbours, tenants, staff. That is traditional. It would have been a happy occasion – had it not been for the arrival, with a party from another house, of the woman Clarissa Vigo. When I set eyes on her ... well, you may imagine. But one has to be civil. I was not going to spoil my only son's most important day.

And so far as I was aware, nothing untoward occurred. The party proceeded. Everyone enjoyed it. My son was a fine young man and took over his duties with pride.

But I had reckoned without the powers of evil. On that evening, Clarissa Vigo took my son. I mean that. She took him by force of persuasion, she seduced him, however you wish to describe what happened. He was lost to me and to everything else here. He was under her influence and her sway and he married her.

Clearly she had been planning this for years. Within six months of that terrible day, my mother-in-law was dead and I had been dismissed from here, given a small farmhouse on the farthest side of the estate and a few sticks of furniture. I had an inheritance of a personal income from my husband which could not be taken from me but otherwise I had nothing. Nothing. This house was barred to me. I did not see my son. Her reign was absolute. And then the plunder began – things were removed, sold, thrown away and otherwise disposed of, things she did not care for, and without a word of protest from my son. She took charge of everything. She had what she had wanted and schemed for, for so many years. In the midst of it all, the Venetian picture was among the things she got rid of and I knew nothing. I knew nothing until later. The final tragedy came five years later. She and my son went out hunting, as they did almost every day throughout the winter. My husband had never hunted – he loathed field sports, though he allowed shooting of vermin on the estate. He was a gentle man but she stamped upon any streak of gentleness there may have been in his son. As they hunted one November day, in jumping a fence in the wood, she fell and was killed outright, and in the crashing fall disturbed a decayed tree, which was uprooted and came down, killing another horseman and injuring my son. He lived, Dr Parmitter. He lived, paralysed in every limb, for seven years. He lived to regret bitterly what he had done, to regret his marriage, to come out from under her possession and to ask me to forgive him. Of course I did so without hesitation and I returned to live here and to care for him until he died.

And I made it my work to restore the house and everything in it to the way it had been and to undo every single change she had made, to throw out every hideous modern thing with which she had filled this place. I brought back the servants she had dismissed. It was my single-minded determination to obliterate her from Hawdon and to leave it in as near the state in which I had first seen it as I could.

I succeeded very well. I was helped by the loyal people here, who flocked back, and by friends and neighbours who sought out so many items and brought them back here, over time.

But one thing I could never trace. The Venetian picture mattered to me because ... because my husband was trapped there. My husband lived – lives, lives – within that picture.

'I sought after it for years', the Countess continued, 'and then it was found for me in an auctioneer's catalogue. I commissioned someone to attend the sale and buy it for me no matter what it cost. But as you know, things went wrong at the last minute, you bought it because my representative was not there and you would not sell it to him afterwards. That was your privilege. But I was angry, Dr Parmitter. I was angry and distressed and frustrated. I wanted that picture, my picture, and I have continued to want it for all these years. But you had disappeared. We could not trace the buyer of the picture.'

'No. In those days, I dealt rather a lot and I bid and bought under aliases – all dealers do. The auction houses of course know one's true identity but they never disclose that sort of information.'

'You were Mr Thomas Joiner and Mr Joiner was never to be found. And so the matter rested. Of course I continued to hope, and friends and searchers continued to keep their eyes and ears open, but my picture had vanished together with Mr Joiner.'

'Until you chanced to see my photograph in a magazine.'

'Indeed. I cannot begin to describe to you my feelings on seeing the picture there – the sense of an ending, the realization that at last, at long last, my husband would in a very real sense return home to me.'

In a macabre comparison, it flashed through my mind that, to the Countess, wanting the picture back was like wanting to receive an urn full of his cremated ashes. Whatever had happened, to her he was as present in the Venetian painting as he would have been in some funereal jar.

'I invited you here with the greatest of pleasure,' she said now. 'And I felt that you had every right to hear the full story and to meet me, to see this place. I could have employed some envoy – and hope that it was a more efficient one than the last time – but that was not the way I wanted to bring about a conclusion to this most important business.'

'A conclusion?' I said with feigned innocence. Inside me I could feel determination, that absolute and steadfast steel resolve. It was unlike me. The man you know as Theo Parmitter would most likely have not so much sold back but given back the Venetian painting. But something had possessed me there. I was not the man you knew and know.

'I mean to have my picture. You may name your price, Dr Parmitter.'

'But it is not for sale.'

'Of course it is for sale. Only a fool would refuse to sell when he could name his price. You have been a dealer in pictures.'

'No longer. The Venetian picture and all the others I have chosen to keep are my permanent collection. I value them quite beyond money. As I said, it is not for sale. I would be happy to provide you with a very good photograph. I would be glad for you to visit me in Cambridge to see it at any time to suit you. But I will never sell.'

Two points of bright colour had appeared on her high cheekbones and two points of brightness in the centre of her already piercing blue eyes. She was sitting upright, straight-backed, her face a white mask of anger.

'I think that perhaps you do not understand me clearly,' she said now. 'I will have my picture. I mean it to come to me.'

'Then I am sorry.'

'You do not need it. It means nothing to you. Or only in the sense that it pleases you as a decoration on your wall.'

'No. It means more than that. You must remember that I have had it for some years.'

'That is of no consequence.'

'It is to me.'

There was a long silence, during which she stared at me unflinchingly. Her expression was quite terrifying. She had not struck me in any case as a warm woman, though she had spoken of her sufferings and her feelings and I had sympathized with her. But there was a cold ruthlessness, a passionate single-mindedness about her now which alarmed me.

'If you do not let me have the picture, you will live to regret your decision, regret it more than you have ever regretted anything.'

'Oh, there is little in my life that I regret, Countess.' I kept a tone of lightness and good humour in my voice which I most assuredly did not feel.

'The picture is better here. It will be quite harmless.'

'How on earth could it be anything else?'

'You have heard my story.'

I stood up. 'I regret that I must leave here today, Countess, and leave without acceding to your request. I found your story interesting and curious and I am grateful to you for your hospitality. I hope you may live out your days in this beautiful spot with the peace of mind you deserve after your sufferings.'

'I will never have peace of mind, never rest, never be content, until the picture is returned to me.'

I turned away. But as I walked towards the door,

the Countess said quietly, 'And nor will you, Dr
Parmitter. Nor will you.'

SEVEN

'YOU WILL FEEL better for having told all this to me,' I said to Theo. He had his head back, his eyes closed, and when he had finished speaking, he had drained his whisky glass and set it down.

It was late. He looked suddenly much older, I thought, but when he opened his eyes again and looked at me there was something new there, an expression of relief. He seemed very calm.

'Thank you, Oliver. I am grateful to you. You have done me more good than you may know.'

I left him with a light heart and took a turn or two around the college court. But tonight, all was quiet and still, there were no shadows, no whisperings, no footsteps, no faces at any lighted windows. No fear.

I slept at once and deeply, and I remember, as I dropped down into the soft cushions of oblivion, praying that Theo would do the same. I thought it most likely.

❦

I woke in the small hours of the morning. It was pitch black and silent but as I came to, I heard the chapel clock strike three. I was sweating and my heart was racing. I had had no nightmares – no dreams of any kind – but I was in a state of abject fear. I could barely take deep breaths to calm myself. I got up and drank water, lay down again, but immediately, I was seized with the need to go down and check on Theo. The message in my head would not be ignored or dismissed. I rinsed my head under the cold tap and rubbed it vigorously dry to try and get some grip on myself and think rationally, but I could not. I was terrified, not for myself but for Theo. The story he had told me was vivid in my mind and although unburdening himself of it had clearly eased his mind greatly, I sensed that, in some terrible way, it was unfinished, that there would be more strange, dark happenings which made no sense, could not be, yet were.

I could not rest. I went down the dark staircase and along to Theo's set. All was quiet. I put my head to the door and listened intently but there was no sound at all. I waited, wondering if I should knock, but it was bitterly cold and I had only a thin dressing gown. I turned to go but, as I did so, it occurred to me that Theo might well not lock his door. He was old and unable to move far, and looked after well by the college. I did not know how he would summon help if he were ill and could not reach the telephone.

I reached my hand out to try the door. As I touched it, there was a harsh and horrible cry from within followed by a single loud crash.

I turned the knob and found that the door was indeed unlocked. I pushed my way in and switched on the lights.

Theo was lying on his back in the entrance to the sitting room, in his night clothes. His face was twisted slightly to the left, his mouth looked as if he were about to speak. His eyes were wide open and staring and they had in them a look I will never forget to my dying day, a look of such horror, such terror, such appalled realization and recognition that it was dreadful to see. I knelt down and touched him. There was no breath, no pulse. He was dead. For a second, I assumed that the crash I had heard was of his own fall, but then I saw that on the floor a few yards away from him lay the Venetian picture. The wire, which I knew had been strong and firm the previous evening, was intact, the hook on the wall in its place. Nothing had snapped or broken, sending it crashing down and Theo had not knocked against it, he had not reached it before he fell.

There were two things I knew I had to do. Obviously, I had to call the lodge, wake the college, set the usual business in motion. But before I did that, I had to do another thing. I dreaded it but I would never be able to rest again until I had, and, also, I felt I owed this last favour to my old tutor. I had to find out.I lifted up the picture and took it into the study where I propped it against the bookcase and turned the lamp directly onto it.

I drew in my breath and looked at the picture, knowing what I would find there.

But I did not. I searched every inch of that canvas. I looked at every face, in the crowd, in the gondolas, in the windows of the houses, in corners, down alleyways, barely visible. There was no Theo.

No face remotely resembled his. I saw the young man I took to be the Countess's young husband, and the figure in the white silk mask with the plume of white feathers in her hair which I supposed was Clarissa Vigo. But of Theo, thank God, thank God, there was no image. I realized that in all probability, he had woken, felt unwell, got up and had his fatal stroke or heart attack. In crashing to the ground, he had shaken floor and walls – he was a heavy man – and the picture had been disturbed and fallen also.

Breaking out in a sweat again, but this time of relief, I went to the telephone on Theo's desk and dialled the night porter.

❧❦

It was a desperately sad few days and I missed Theo greatly. The college chapel was packed and overflowing for his funeral, the oration one of the best I had ever heard and afterwards everyone spoke fondly of him. I was still shocked, my mind still full of our last hours together. From time to time, one thing came to my mind to trouble me. I had satisfied myself, I am pretty sure, that Theo's death had had nothing to do with the story he had told me, with the

Venetian picture or indeed with anything shocking or unexplained. Yet I could not forget the look of terror on his dead face, the horrified expression in his open eyes, the way his arm was outstretched. The picture had fallen, and although there was a perfectly sensible explanation for that, it worried me.

I left Cambridge with a heavy heart. I would never again sit in those comfortable rooms, talking over a fire and a whisky, hearing his sound views on so many subjects, his humorous asides and his sharp but never cruel comments on his fellows.

But I could not remain overly sad or troubled for long. I had work to get back to, but even more I had Anne. I had told Theo in the first few minutes after my arrival that I was engaged to be married to Anne Fernleigh – not a fellow scholar in medieval English but a barrister – beautiful, accomplished, fun, a few years younger than I was. The perfect wife. Theo had wished me well and asked that I would take her to meet him soon. I had said that I would. And now I could not. It cast a shadow. Of course, one wants two people one cares for to meet and to care for one another in turn.

I had told her of Theo's death, of course – the

reason that I had stayed on longer than planned, and now, as we sat in her flat after a good dinner, I told her in turn the story of the Venetian picture and of the old Countess. She listened intently, but at the end, smiled and said, 'I'm sorry I won't meet your old tutor for I have a feeling I would have liked him, but I can't say I'm sorry not to be meeting the picture. It sounds horrible.'

'It's rather fine, actually.'

'Not the art – I'm sure you may be right. The story. The whole business of ...' she shuddered.

'It's a tale. A good one, but just a tale. It needn't trouble you.'

'It troubled him.'

'Oh, not so very much. It was a story he wanted to tell over a whisky and a good fire on a cold night. Forget it. We've more important things to discuss. I have something I want to ask you.'

Since my days with Theo and his sudden death, I had had one thought. I do not know why, but it seemed very important to me that instead of marrying the following summer, planning everything in a leisurely way and making a fuss of it, we should marry now, straight away.

'I know it will mean we marry quietly, without

all the razzmatazz and perhaps that will disappoint you. But I don't want us to wait. Theo's death made me realize that we should seize life – and he was a lonely man, you know. No family other than a Cambridge college. Oh, he was contented enough but he was lonely and a college full of strangers, however warmly disposed, is not a wife and children.'

But to my surprise, Anne said she had no problem at all in giving up plans for a lavish wedding and in being married quietly, with just our family and closest friends, as soon as it could be arranged.

'It isn't the money you spend and the fuss you make – a marriage is about other things that are far more serious and lasting. Think of that poor old Countess – think of the wretched other woman. We are very fortunate. We should never forget it.'

I never would. I never will. I could not have been happier and I had a good feeling that Theo would have agreed, and approved. I felt his blessing upon us and his benign presence hovering about us as we made our preparations.

The only hesitation I had was when Anne determined that, even though work meant we could not now take the long honeymoon in Kenya that we had planned, we should manage a long weekend away and asked if we might spend it in Venice.

'I went once when I was fourteen,' she said, 'and I sensed something magical but I was too young to know what it was — I think one can be too young for Venice.'

'Well perhaps we should save it for a longer visit in that case,' I said, 'and go down to the south of France.'

'No, it won't be warm enough there yet. Venice. Please?'

I shook off any forebodings and made the booking. Superstitions and stories were not going to cast their long shadow over the first days of our marriage and I realized that in fact I was greatly looking forward to visiting the city again. Venice is beautiful. Venice is magical. Venice is like nowhere else, in the real world or the worlds of invention. I remembered the first time I visited it, as a young man taking a few months out to travel, and emerging from the railway station to that astonishing sight — streets which were water. The first ride on the vaporetto down the Grand Canal, the first glimpse of San Giorgio

Maggiore rising out of the mist, the first sight of the pigeons rising like a ghostly cloud above the cathedral in St Mark's Square, and of those turrets and spires touched with gold and gleaming in the sun. Walks through squares where all you hear are the sounds of many footsteps on stone, because there are no motor vehicles, hours spent at café tables on the quiet Giudecca, the cry of the fish-sellers in the early morning, the graceful arch of the Rialto Bridge, the faces of the locals, old and young men and women with those memorable, ancient Venetian features – the prominent nose, the hauteur of expression, the red hair.

The more I thought about the city in those days leading up to the wedding, the more my pulse quickened with the anticipation of seeing it again, and this time with Anne. Venice filled my dreams and was there when I woke. I found myself searching out books about her – the novels by Henry James and Edith Wharton and others which caught the moods so vividly. Once or twice, I thought about Theo's picture and its strange story, but now I was merely intrigued, wondering where the tale had originated and how long ago. When we got back, I meant to look up Hawdon and the Countess's family. Perhaps we would even take a few days in Yorkshire later in the year. The real settings of stories always hold a fascination.

Anne and I were married two weeks later, on a day of brilliant, warm sunshine – surely a good omen for our happiness. We had a celebratory lunch with our families and a couple of friends – I wished Theo could have been there - and by late afternoon, we were en route for our honeymoon in Venice.

EIGHT

T O GIVE MYSELF something to do while I wait here, I write what I am beginning to fear must be the end of this story, and with such grief and anguish, such bewilderment and fear, that I can barely hold the pen. I am writing to give myself something, something to do in these long and dreadful hours when all hope is lost and yet I still must hope, for once hope is extinguished, there is nothing else left.

I am sitting in the room of our hotel. The balcony windows are open wide onto this quiet corner of the city. Just now, through the darkness, from one of the houses opposite the hotel I heard a man singing arias from Puccini and Mozart. Cats yowl suddenly. I write and I do not understand what I am writing or why but they say that a fear, like a nightmare, written down is exorcised. Writing should calm me as I wait. When I stop writing, I pace up and down the room, before returning to this small table in front of the window. The telephone is at my right hand. Any moment, any moment now, it will ring with the news I am desperate to hear.

How do I describe what happened when I barely know? How to explain something for which there is no explanation? I can as soon convey the pain I am feeling.

But I must, I have to. I cannot let the story remain unfinished or I shall go mad. For now it is my story, mine and Anne's, we have somehow become a part of this horrible nightmare.

We had been less than twenty-four hours in the city when Anne discovered that there was, as there so often is, a festival in honour of one of Venice's hundreds of saints, with a procession, fireworks, dancing in the square.

I said that we would go but that I was adamant that if there was to be any dressing-up, any tradition of wearing masks, we would not join in. I did not believe in Theo's story and yet it, together with the strange things that had happened to me in

Cambridge and his subsequent death, had made me anxious nevertheless, anxious and suspicious. It was irrational but I felt that I needed to stay on the side of good luck, not court the bad.

The first hour or two of the festival was tremendous fun. The streets were full of people on their way to join the procession, the shops had some sort of special cakes baking and the smell filled the night air. There were drummers and dancers and people playing pipes on every corner, and many of the balconies had flags and garlands hanging from them. I am trying to remember how it felt, to be lighthearted, to be full of happiness, walking through the city with Anne, such a short time ago.

St Mark's Square was thronged and there was music coming from every side. We walked along the Riva degli Schiavoni and back, moving slowly with the long procession, and as we returned, the fireworks began over the water, lighting the sky and the ancient buildings and the canal itself in greens and blues, reds and golds in turn. Showers of crystals and silver and gold dust shot up into the air, the rockets soared. It was spectacular. I was so happy to be a part of it.

We walked along the canal, in and out of the

alleys and squares, until we came down between high buildings again to a spot facing the bridge.

The jetty was thronged with people. All of those who had been processing must have been there and we were pushed and jostled by people trying to get to the front beside the canal, where the gondolas were lined up waiting to take people to the festivities on the opposite bank. The fireworks were still exploding in all directions so that every few minutes there was a collective cry or sigh of wonder from the crowd. And then I noticed that some of them were wearing the costumes of the carnival: the ancient Venetian figures of the Old Woman, the Fortune Teller, the Doctor, the Barber, the Man with the Monkey, Pulcinello, and Death with his scythe mingled among us, their faces concealed by low hats and masks and paint, eyes gleaming here and there. I was suddenly stricken with panic. I had not meant to be here. I wanted to leave, urgently, to go back to our quiet square and sit at the café over a drink in the balmy evening. I turned to Anne.

But she was not at my side. Somehow, she had been hidden from me by the ever-changing crowd. I pushed my way between bodies urgently, calling her name. I turned to see if she was behind me. And as I turned, the blood stopped in my veins. My heart itself seemed to cease beating. My mouth was dry and my tongue felt swollen and I could not speak Anne's name.

I glimpsed, a yard or two away, a figure wearing a white silk mask studded with sequins and with a white plume of feathers in her dark hair. I caught her eyes, dark and huge and full of hatred.

I struggled to my left, towards the alleyway, away from the water, away from the gondolas rocking and swaying, away from the masks and the figures and the brilliant lights of the fireworks that kept exploding and cascading down again towards the dark water. I lost sight of the woman and when I looked back again she had gone.

I ran then, ran and ran, calling out to Anne, shouting for help, screaming in the end as I searched frantically through all the twists and turns of Venice for my wife.

I came back to the hotel. I alerted the police. I was forced to wait to give them Anne's description. They said that visitors to Venice get lost every day, especially in a crowd, that until it was daylight they had little hope of finding her but that she would be most likely to return here on her own, or perhaps in the care of someone local, that perhaps she had fallen or become ill. They were stolid. They tried to reassure me. They left, telling me to wait here for Anne.

But I cannot wait.

I have to leave this wretched story and go out again, I will go mad until I find her. Because I saw the woman, the woman in the white silk mask with the white plumes in her hair, the woman in the story, the woman desperate for revenge. I believe in her now. I have seen. Why she would want to harm Anne I have no idea, but she is a destroyer of happiness, one whom even death cannot stop in her desire to haunt and hurt.

I will do whatever is necessary – and perhaps I am the only person who can – to put an end to it all.

NINE

T IS LEFT TO ME, Anne, to end this story. Will there be an ending? Oh, there has to be, there must. Such evil surely cannot retain its power for ever?

In the crowd of people on the landing stage beside the water, I had felt myself at first jostled and pushed by a number of people who were trying to surge forward — indeed, I feared for a child at the very edge of the canal and pulled her away in case she fell in. I almost lost my own balance, but I felt a hand on my arm, helping me to right myself. The only unnerving thing was that the hand gripped me so hard it was painful and I had to wrench myself hard to get away. I caught a glimpse of someone, of a malevolent glance that made me shudder, and saw a hand reached out again towards me. But then I was being taken forward by the crowd trying to go in the opposite direction, away from the crowd by the water and I let myself go with them, up the narrow walk between the high houses and onto one of the small bridges over a side canal.

Then, the procession, which I had thought disbanded, re-formed, a band began to play and we were all walking together to the music, towards the Rialto and over it and on and on, and I felt myself caught up in the scene, laughing and clapping and occasionally looking back at the fireworks still bursting into the night sky. It was exhilarating, it was fun. I was unaware of where we were walking but quite happy, confident that, in a short time, I would separate myself from the others, and turn back.

But for one reason or another I did not and then we were far away, the band still playing, children banging toy drums, through streets, across bridges, into squares. The Venice I knew was left far behind. And then I slipped on an uneven stretch of the pavement, and fell, and in doing so, put my weight on my arm. I heard a crack and felt the pain, I let out a cry. Someone stopped. Someone else shouted. People bent over me. I was surrounded, helped, admonished, and everyone was jabbering in fast Italian which I could not understand. I was suddenly and violently sick and the sky whirled and then it was coming down on my head.

There is little else to tell. I was taken into a near-by house and a doctor was fetched. I had not, he decided, broken my arm, I had bruised it badly and cut my hand and they looked after me very kindly. I was bandaged, given an injection against infections, swallowed painkillers. By now, it was two in the morning and I wrote down and gave to one of those looking after me my name and the telephone number of the hotel. But I felt nauseous again and the doctor insisted that I should lie down and sleep, that everything would be done. I would be moved the next morning.

I did sleep. The pain in my arm and hand did not wake me for some hours, and by then I was feeling better in myself and able to drink some good strong coffee and eat a soft bread roll with butter.

What happened next made me laugh. I wonder, when I will laugh again?

I was coaxed into a wheelchair belonging to the grandmother of the family, and trundled through the morning streets of Venice in the sunshine, my bandaged arm resting proudly on my lap, back to our hotel and my husband.

Except that Oliver was not there. He had gone out to search for me again, they said, he had slipped past the night porter in the early hours, distraught. At first, no one reported having seen him but, later that day, the police, who had switched from looking for me to looking for him with some irritation at accident-prone visitors, told me that a gondolier, up early to wash out his craft, reported having seen a man answering to Oliver's description. But at first I dismissed it, saying that it could not have been Oliver. He had been reported as walking between two men who had their hands on his arms and seemed to be making him get into another gondola, farther up the jetty, against his will. Oliver would have been alone.

The police took it more seriously but could see no reason at all, if it had been Oliver with two men, why he should have been taken anywhere against his will. He did not look rich, our hotel was not one of the grandest, his wallet was still in the room and the watch he always wore was a plain steel one without great value.

I did not buy any theories of kidnap, ransom or

the mafia. Italian police seem obsessed with all three but I knew they were far from the mark.

I knew. I know.

I read the story Oliver had left. I read everything twice, slowly and carefully, I crawled over it, if you like, looking for a message, an explanation.

I came back to London alone.

That was a fortnight ago. Nothing happened. There was no news. In the first few days the Venetian police telephoned me. The Inspector spoke good English.

'Signora, we have revised our opinion. This man the *gondoliere* saw with the others ... we think it is not probable to be your husband, after all. Our theory is now, he slip and fall into the Grande Canale. He was out in the dark, the ground there is often wet.'

'But you would have found his body?'

'Not yet, not found yet. But yes, the body will be washed up later or sooner and we will call you at once.'

'Will I have to come to identify him?'

'*Si.* I am very sorry but yes, it is necessary.'

I thanked him and then I wept. I wept for what felt like hours, until my body ached, my throat was sore and I had no tears left. And I dreaded having to travel back to Venice to see Oliver's dead – his drowned – body, when the time came. I had been told about the look of death by water.

I decided I must go back to work, if only in the office. I must have something to occupy my mind and it was a relief to sit reading through complex, dry, legal phraseology for hours at a time. If my thoughts turned to Venice, the black filthy waters of the Grand Canal, the next flight I would take there, I went out and walked for miles through London, trying to tire myself out.

Two days ago, I had walked from Lincoln's Inn back to our flat. My arm still ached a little and I thought I would take some strong painkillers and try to sleep. The phone was switched through to my office, and when I left there, to my mobile, so I knew I had not missed a call from the police.

The porter in our mansion block told me that he had taken in a parcel and put it upstairs outside the door. I was not expecting anything and it was with some distress that I saw the label addressed to Oliver. Taped to the outside of the parcel was an envelope – the whole had been delivered by courier.

I took it inside. The sun was shining in through

the tall windows. I opened one of them and heard a blackbird singing its heart out on the plane tree outside. I took off my coat and riffled through the other post, which was of no interest. There was nothing for Oliver.

And so I peeled the envelope from the parcel and opened it. I did not believe, by then, you see, that Oliver would ever return to open it. Oliver was dead. Drowned. Before long I would see that, with my own eyes.

The letter was from a firm of solicitors in Cambridge. It enclosed a cheque for a thousand pounds, left to Oliver by his old tutor, Theo, 'to buy himself a present'. I had to wipe the tears out of my eyes before reading on, to learn that the letter came with an item which Dr Parmitter had also left to Oliver in his will.

It is very strange, but as I began to cut off the brown paper, I had no idea as to what the item could possibly be. I should have known, of course I should. I should have taken the whole package, unopened, down to the incinerator and burned it, or taken a knife and slashed it to shreds.

Instead, I simply undid the last of the wrapping paper and looked down at the Venetian picture.

And as I did so, as my heart contracted and my fingers became numb, I smelled, quite unmistakably, the faintest smell of fresh oil paint.

Then, I began the frantic search for my husband.

He was not hard to find. Behind the crowd in their masks and cloaks and tricorn hats, behind the gleaming canal and the rocking gondolas and the flaring torches, I saw the dark alley leading away, and the backs of two large men, heavy and broad-shouldered, cloaked in black, their hands on a man's arms, gripping them. The man was turning his head to look back and to look out, to look beyond the world of the picture, to look at me and his expression was one of terror and of dread. His eyes were begging and imploring me to find him, follow him, rescue him. Get him back.

But it was too late. He was like the others. He had turned into a picture. It took me a little longer to find the woman and then it was only the smallest image, almost hidden in one corner, the gleam of white silk, the sparkle of a sequin, the edge of a white-plumed feather. But she was there. Her arm was outstretched, her finger pointed in Oliver's direction, but her eyes were looking, like his, at me, directly at me, in hideous triumph.

I dropped into a chair before my legs gave way. I had only one hope left. That by taking Oliver, as she had taken the others, surely, surely to God the woman had satisfied her desire for revenge. Who is left? What more can she do? Has she not done enough?

I do not know. I will not know though I cannot say, 'never'. I will live with this fear, this dread, this threat, during all the years ahead until the child I have learned I am expecting, grows up. All I do now is pray and it is always the same prayer – a foolish prayer, of course, since the die is already cast.

I pray that I will not have a son.